KU-616-264

# The Story of
# SHERLOCK HOLMES
## The Famous Detective

Sherlock Holmes and his helpful friend Dr. John Watson are fictional characters created by British writer Sir Arthur Conan Doyle. Doyle published his first novel about the pair, *A Study in Scarlet*, in 1887, and it became very successful. Doyle went on to write fifty-six short stories, as well as three more novels about Holmes's adventures—*The Sign of Four* (1890), *The Hound of the Baskervilles* (1902), and *The Valley of Fear* (1915).

Sherlock Holmes and Dr. Watson have become some of the most famous book characters of all time. Holmes spent most of his time solving mysteries, but he also had a wide array of hobbies, such as playing the violin, boxing, and sword fighting. Watson, a retired army doctor, met Holmes through a mutual friend when Holmes was looking for a roommate. Watson lived with Holmes for several years at 221B Baker Street before marrying and moving out. However, after his marriage, Watson continued to assist Holmes with his cases.

The original versions of the Sherlock Holmes stories are still printed, and many have been made into movies and television shows. Readers continue to be impressed by Holmes's detective methods of observation and scientific reason.

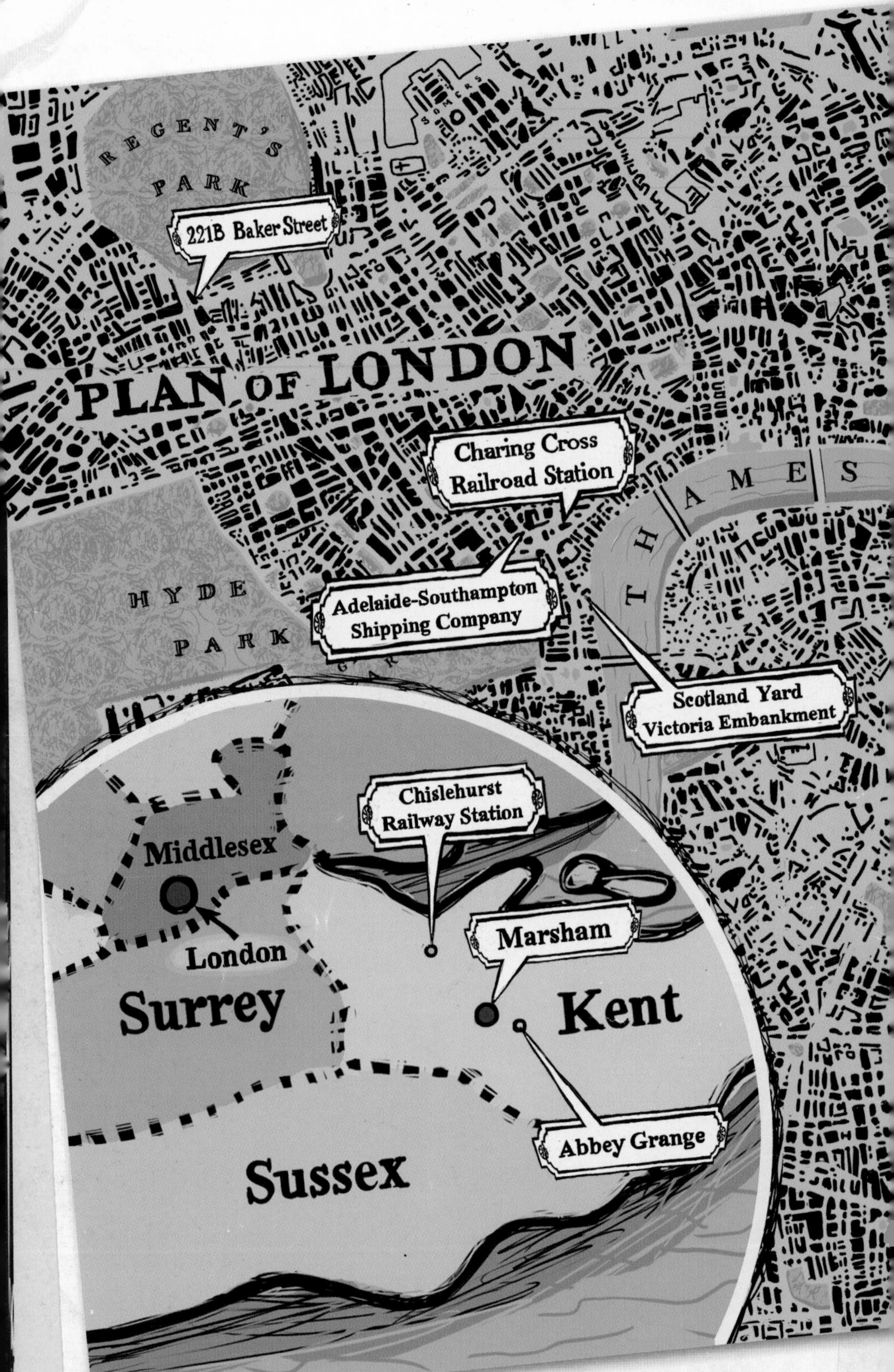

PLAN OF LONDON
REGENT'S PARK
221B Baker Street
SOMERS
Charing Cross Railroad Station
HYDE PARK
Adelaide-Southampton Shipping Company
THAMES
Scotland Yard Victoria Embankment
Chislehurst Railway Station
Middlesex
London
Marsham
Surrey
Kent
Sussex
Abbey Grange

# Character List

Lady Brackenstall

Theresa Wright

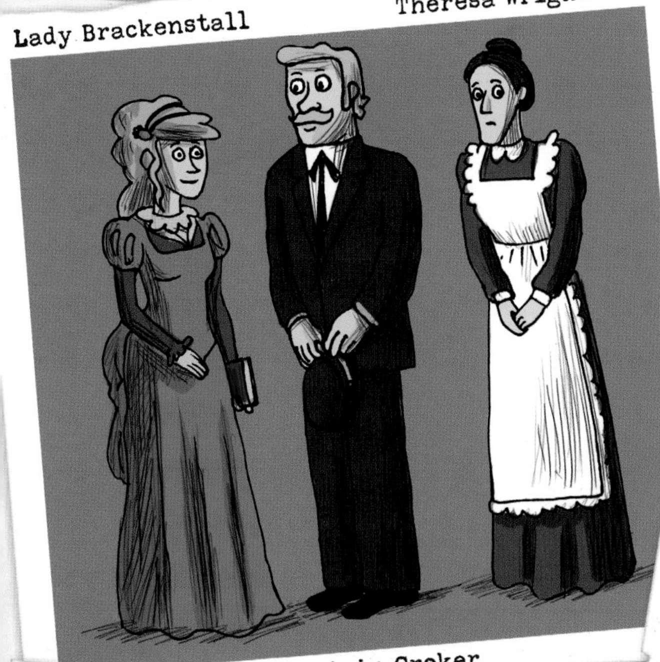

Captain Croker

Shipping Company Manager

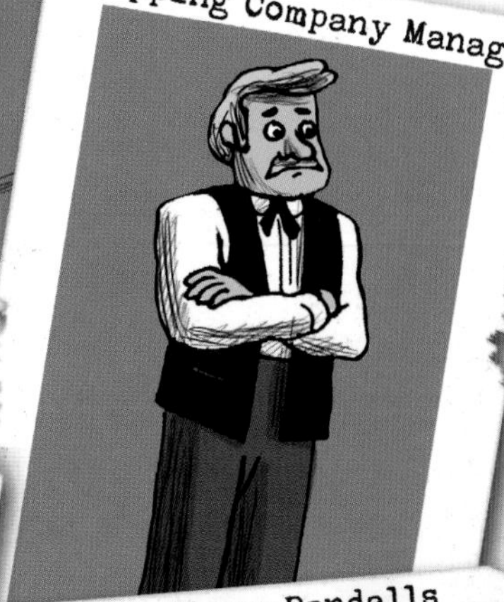

Sherlock Holmes

Inspector Hopkins

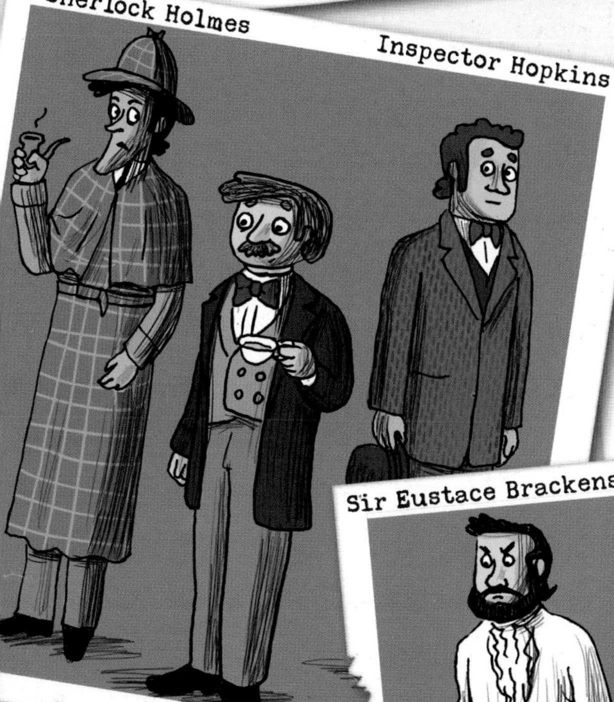

Dr. Watson

The Three Randalls

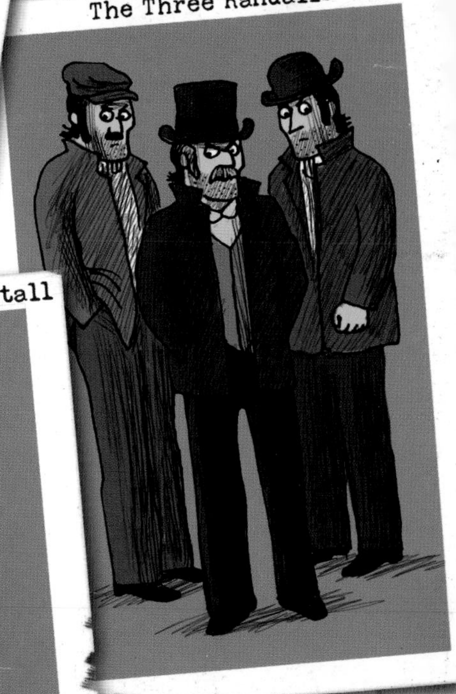

Sir Eustace Brackenstall

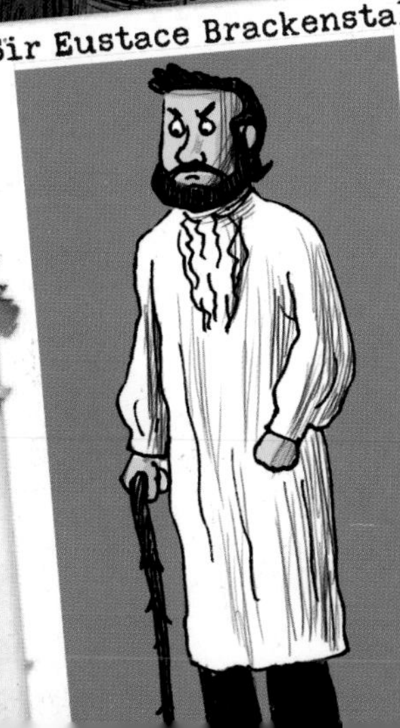

# From the Desk of
# John H. Watson, M.D.

My name is Dr. John H. Watson. For several
years, I have been assisting my friend,
Sherlock Holmes, in solving mysteries
throughout the bustling city of London and
beyond. Holmes is a peculiar man—always
questioning and reasoning his way through
various problems. But when I first met him
in 1878, I was immediately intrigued by his
oddities.

Holmes has always been more daring than I,
and his logical deduction never ceases to
amaze me. I have begun writing down all of the
adventures I have with Holmes. This is one of
those stories.

Sincerely,

Dr. Watson

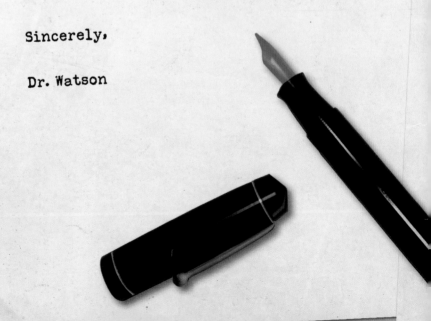

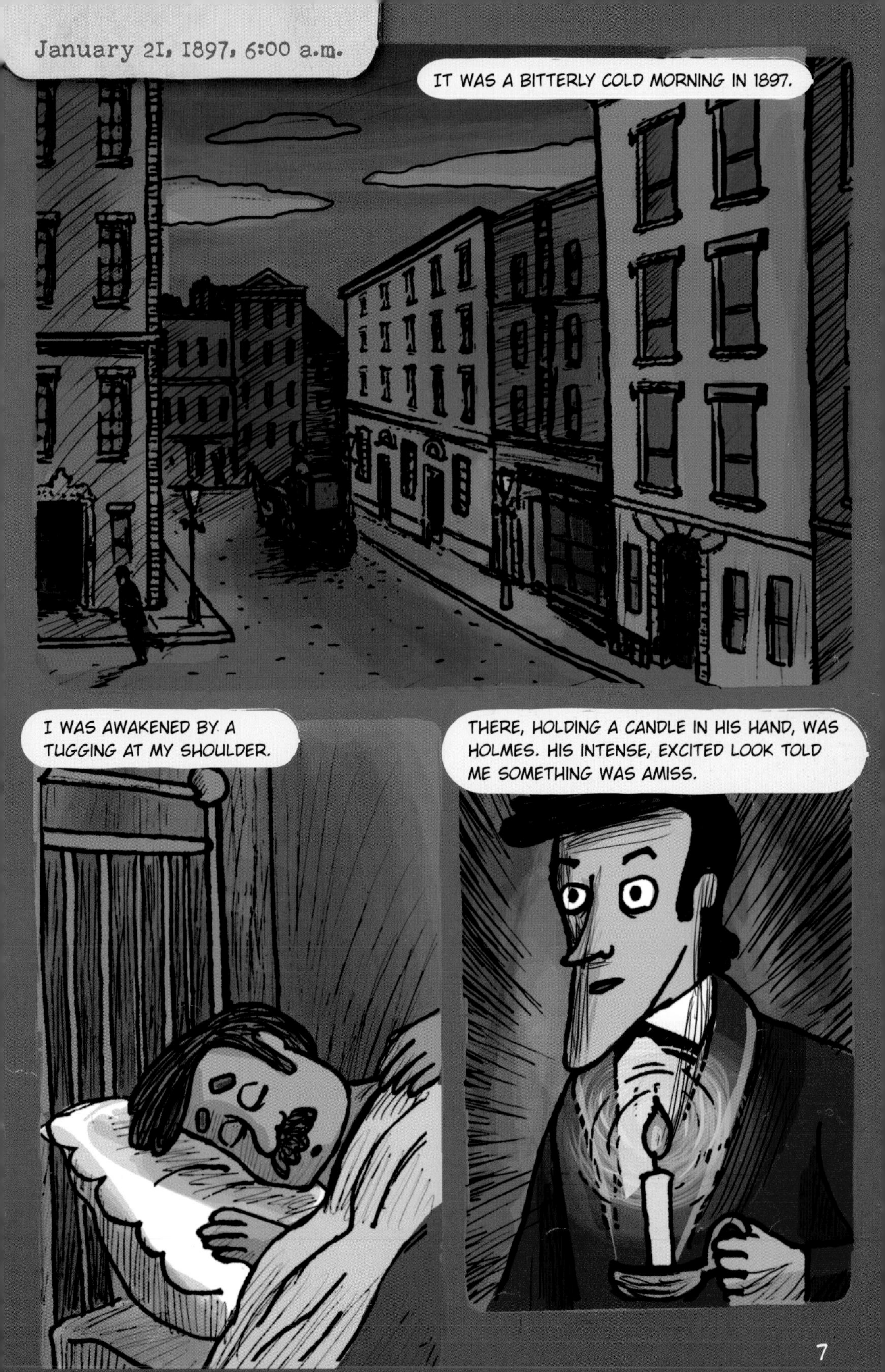
January 21, 1897, 6:00 a.m.
IT WAS A BITTERLY COLD MORNING IN 1897.
I WAS AWAKENED BY A TUGGING AT MY SHOULDER.
THERE, HOLDING A CANDLE IN HIS HAND, WAS HOLMES. HIS INTENSE, EXCITED LOOK TOLD ME SOMETHING WAS AMISS.

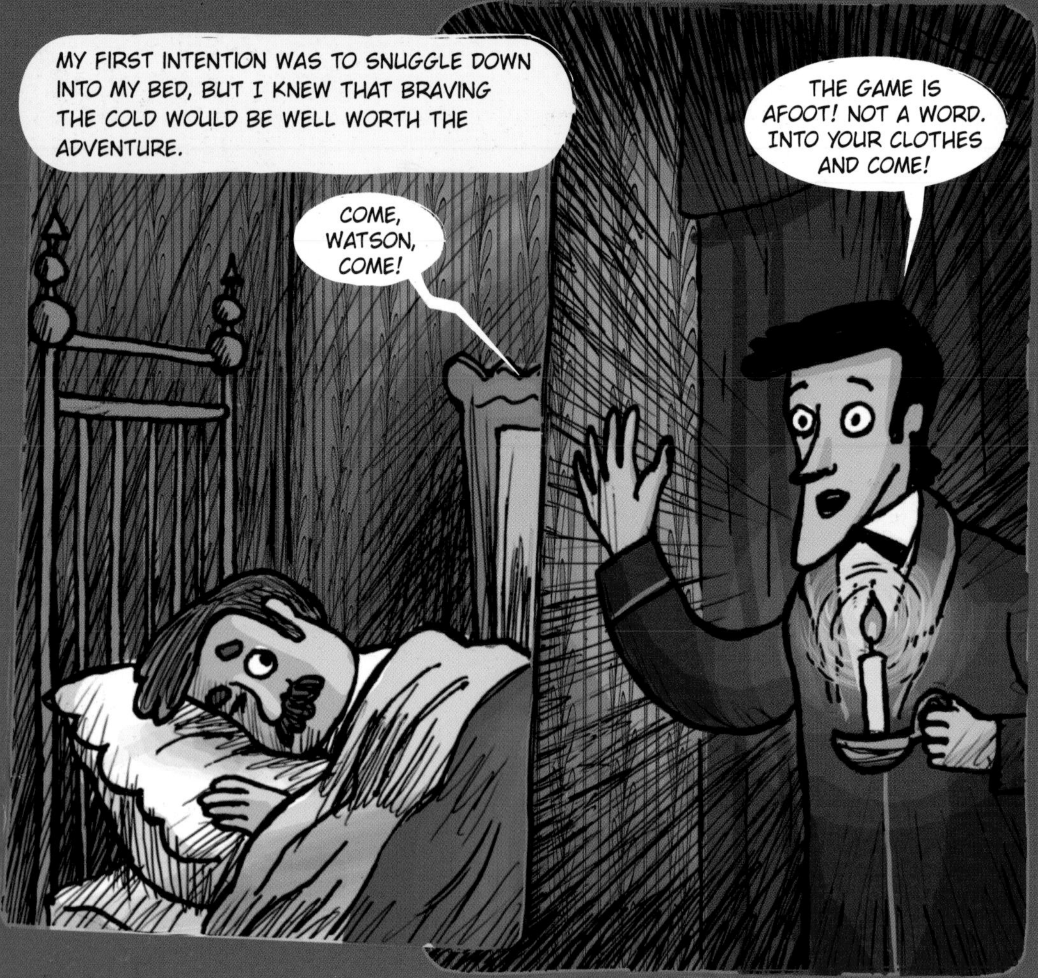
MY FIRST INTENTION WAS TO SNUGGLE DOWN INTO MY BED, BUT I KNEW THAT BRAVING THE COLD WOULD BE WELL WORTH THE ADVENTURE.
COME, WATSON, COME!
THE GAME IS AFOOT! NOT A WORD. INTO YOUR CLOTHES AND COME!

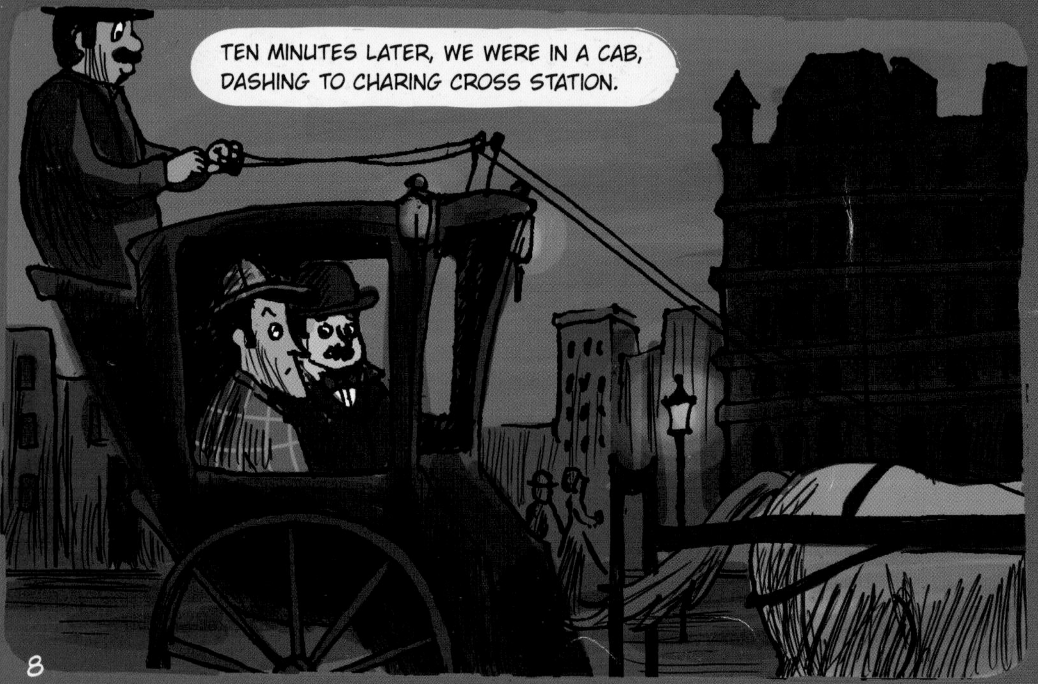
TEN MINUTES LATER, WE WERE IN A CAB, DASHING TO CHARING CROSS STATION.

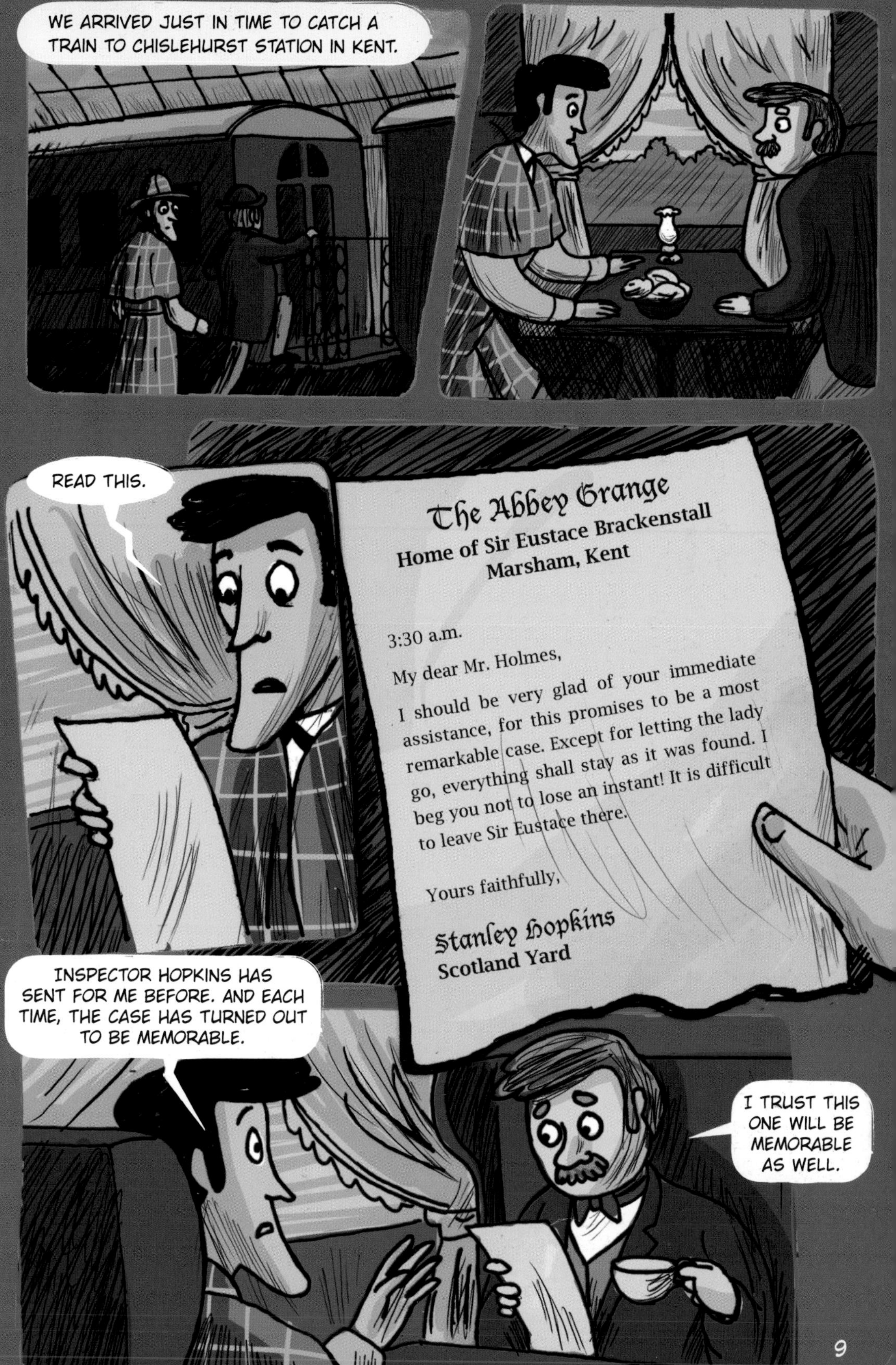
WE ARRIVED JUST IN TIME TO CATCH A TRAIN TO CHISLEHURST STATION IN KENT.
READ THIS.
The Abbey Grange
Home of Sir Eustace Brackenstall
Marsham, Kent
3:30 a.m.
My dear Mr. Holmes,
I should be very glad of your immediate assistance, for this promises to be a most remarkable case. Except for letting the lady go, everything shall stay as it was found. I beg you not to lose an instant! It is difficult to leave Sir Eustace there.
Yours faithfully,
Stanley Hopkins
Scotland Yard
INSPECTOR HOPKINS HAS SENT FOR ME BEFORE. AND EACH TIME, THE CASE HAS TURNED OUT TO BE MEMORABLE.
I TRUST THIS ONE WILL BE MEMORABLE AS WELL.

As he talked, Holmes also noted, with pleasure he said, that his cases involving Scotland Yard had all found their way into my collection of stories. Holmes did, however, object to my bad habit of writing everything as a story. He felt that each case should be a demonstration of the scientific method. He believed that my stories should be more instructive than entertaining. I listened but did not take heed. There is only one Sherlock Holmes. Readers who care to mimic Holmes may take what they want from my stories.

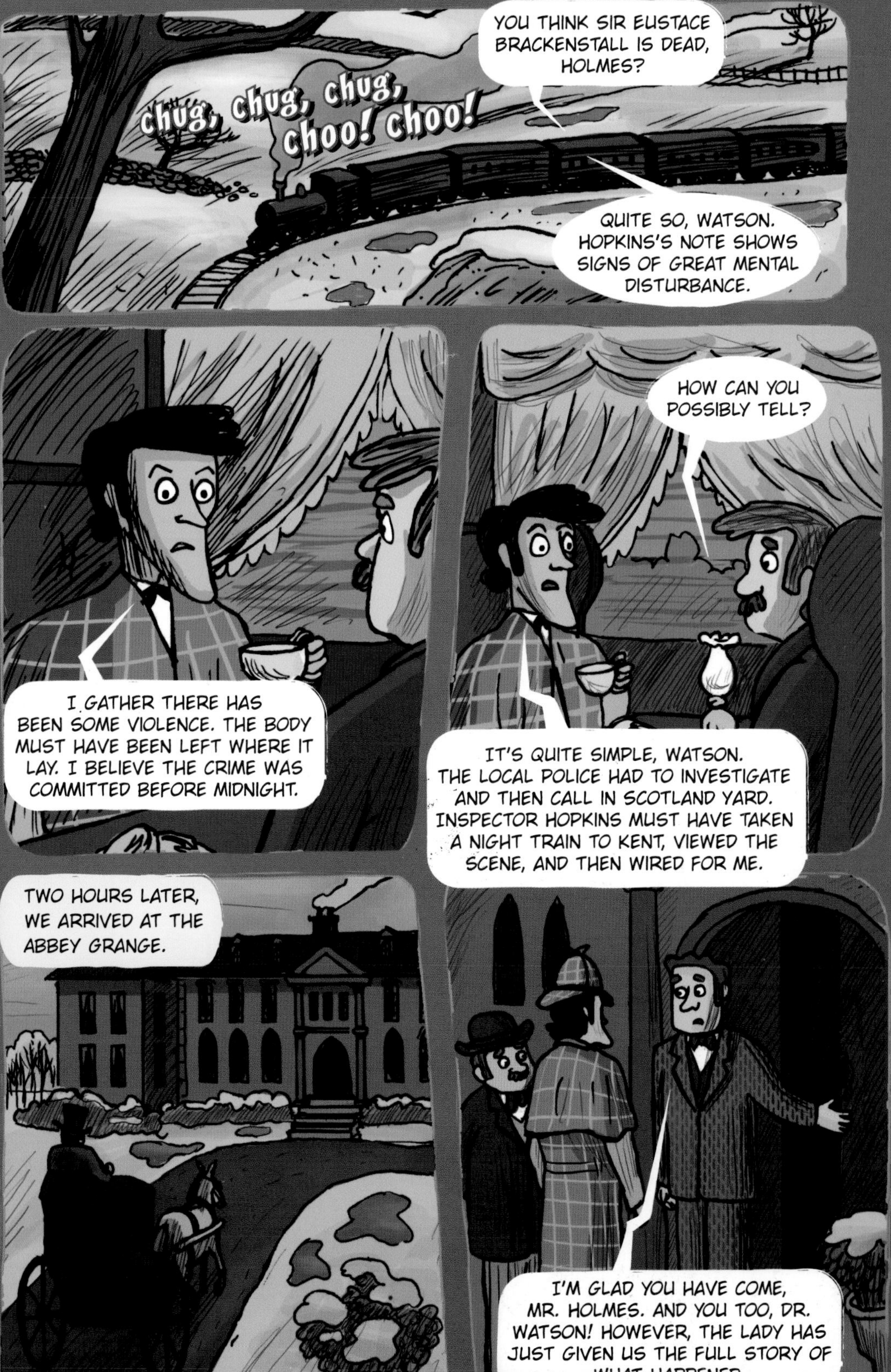
chug, chug, chug, choo! choo!
YOU THINK SIR EUSTACE BRACKENSTALL IS DEAD, HOLMES?
QUITE SO, WATSON. HOPKINS'S NOTE SHOWS SIGNS OF GREAT MENTAL DISTURBANCE.
I GATHER THERE HAS BEEN SOME VIOLENCE. THE BODY MUST HAVE BEEN LEFT WHERE IT LAY. I BELIEVE THE CRIME WAS COMMITTED BEFORE MIDNIGHT.
HOW CAN YOU POSSIBLY TELL?
IT'S QUITE SIMPLE, WATSON. THE LOCAL POLICE HAD TO INVESTIGATE AND THEN CALL IN SCOTLAND YARD. INSPECTOR HOPKINS MUST HAVE TAKEN A NIGHT TRAIN TO KENT, VIEWED THE SCENE, AND THEN WIRED FOR ME.
TWO HOURS LATER, WE ARRIVED AT THE ABBEY GRANGE.
I'M GLAD YOU HAVE COME, MR. HOLMES. AND YOU TOO, DR. WATSON! HOWEVER, THE LADY HAS JUST GIVEN US THE FULL STORY OF WHAT HAPPENED.

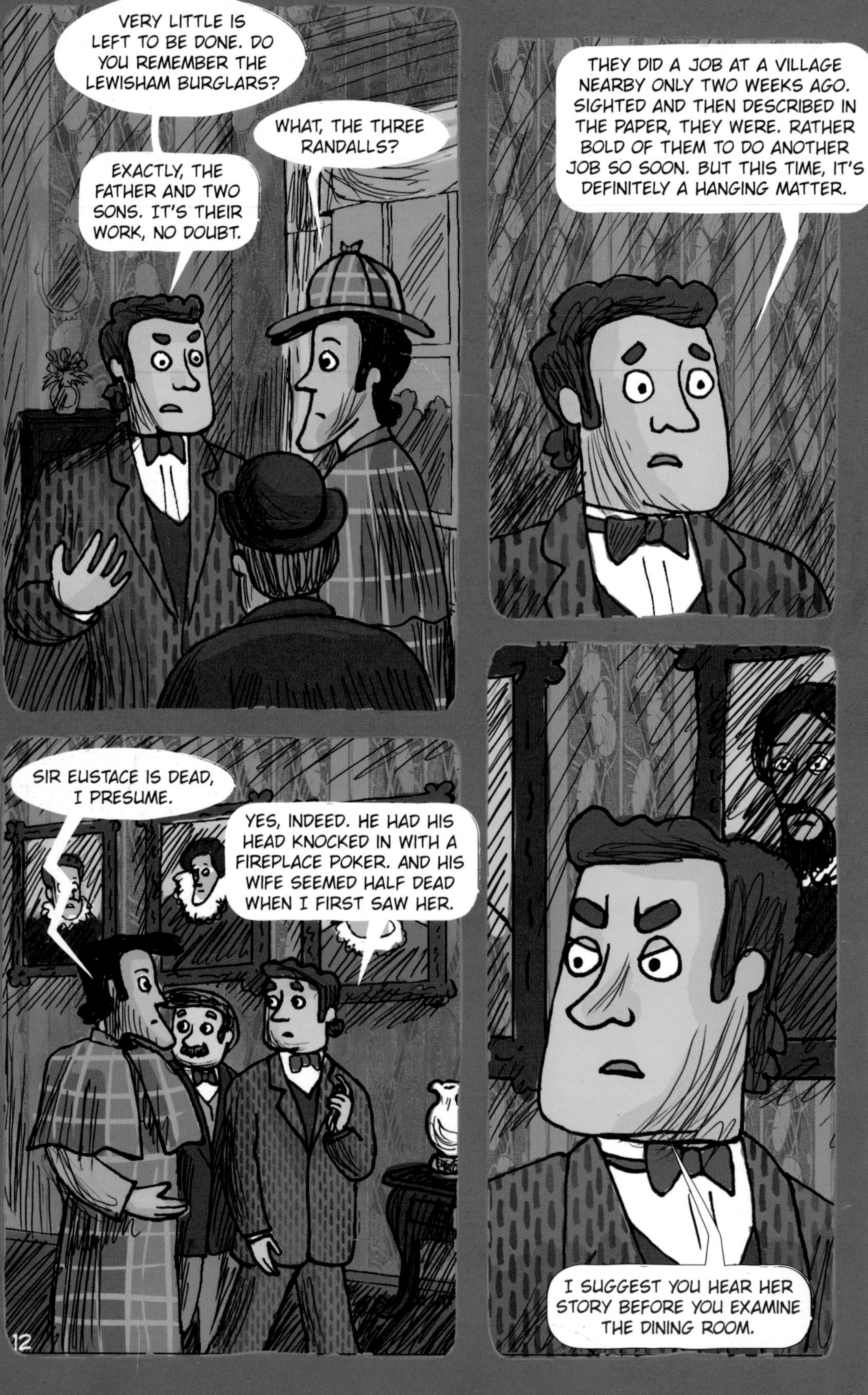
VERY LITTLE IS LEFT TO BE DONE. DO YOU REMEMBER THE LEWISHAM BURGLARS?
WHAT, THE THREE RANDALLS?
EXACTLY, THE FATHER AND TWO SONS. IT'S THEIR WORK, NO DOUBT.
THEY DID A JOB AT A VILLAGE NEARBY ONLY TWO WEEKS AGO. SIGHTED AND THEN DESCRIBED IN THE PAPER, THEY WERE. RATHER BOLD OF THEM TO DO ANOTHER JOB SO SOON. BUT THIS TIME, IT'S DEFINITELY A HANGING MATTER.
SIR EUSTACE IS DEAD, I PRESUME.
YES, INDEED. HE HAD HIS HEAD KNOCKED IN WITH A FIREPLACE POKER. AND HIS WIFE SEEMED HALF DEAD WHEN I FIRST SAW HER.
I SUGGEST YOU HEAR HER STORY BEFORE YOU EXAMINE THE DINING ROOM.

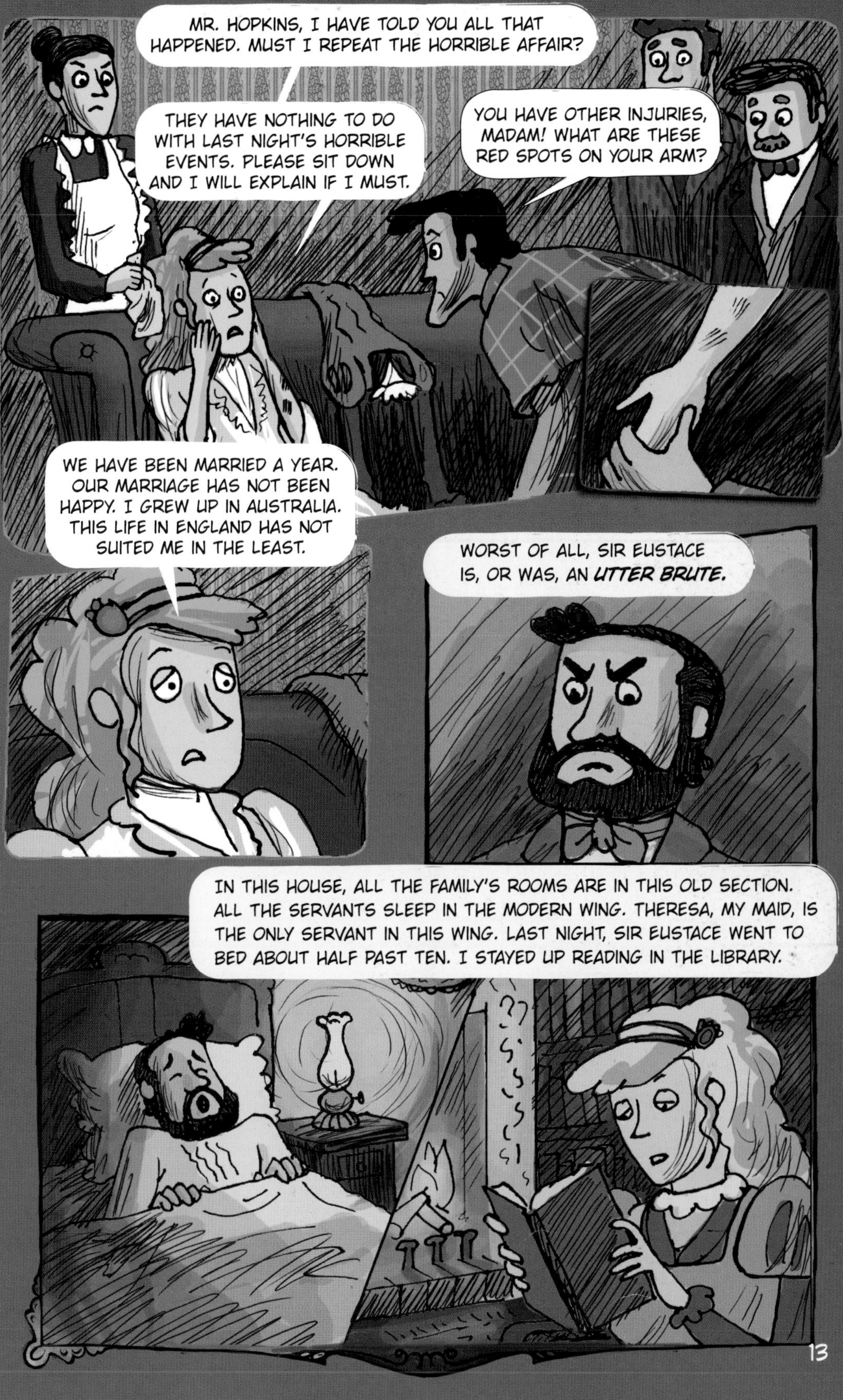
MR. HOPKINS, I HAVE TOLD YOU ALL THAT HAPPENED. MUST I REPEAT THE HORRIBLE AFFAIR?
YOU HAVE OTHER INJURIES, MADAM! WHAT ARE THESE RED SPOTS ON YOUR ARM?
THEY HAVE NOTHING TO DO WITH LAST NIGHT'S HORRIBLE EVENTS. PLEASE SIT DOWN AND I WILL EXPLAIN IF I MUST.
WE HAVE BEEN MARRIED A YEAR. OUR MARRIAGE HAS NOT BEEN HAPPY. I GREW UP IN AUSTRALIA. THIS LIFE IN ENGLAND HAS NOT SUITED ME IN THE LEAST.
WORST OF ALL, SIR EUSTACE IS, OR WAS, AN *UTTER BRUTE.*
IN THIS HOUSE, ALL THE FAMILY'S ROOMS ARE IN THIS OLD SECTION. ALL THE SERVANTS SLEEP IN THE MODERN WING. THERESA, MY MAID, IS THE ONLY SERVANT IN THIS WING. LAST NIGHT, SIR EUSTACE WENT TO BED ABOUT HALF PAST TEN. I STAYED UP READING IN THE LIBRARY.

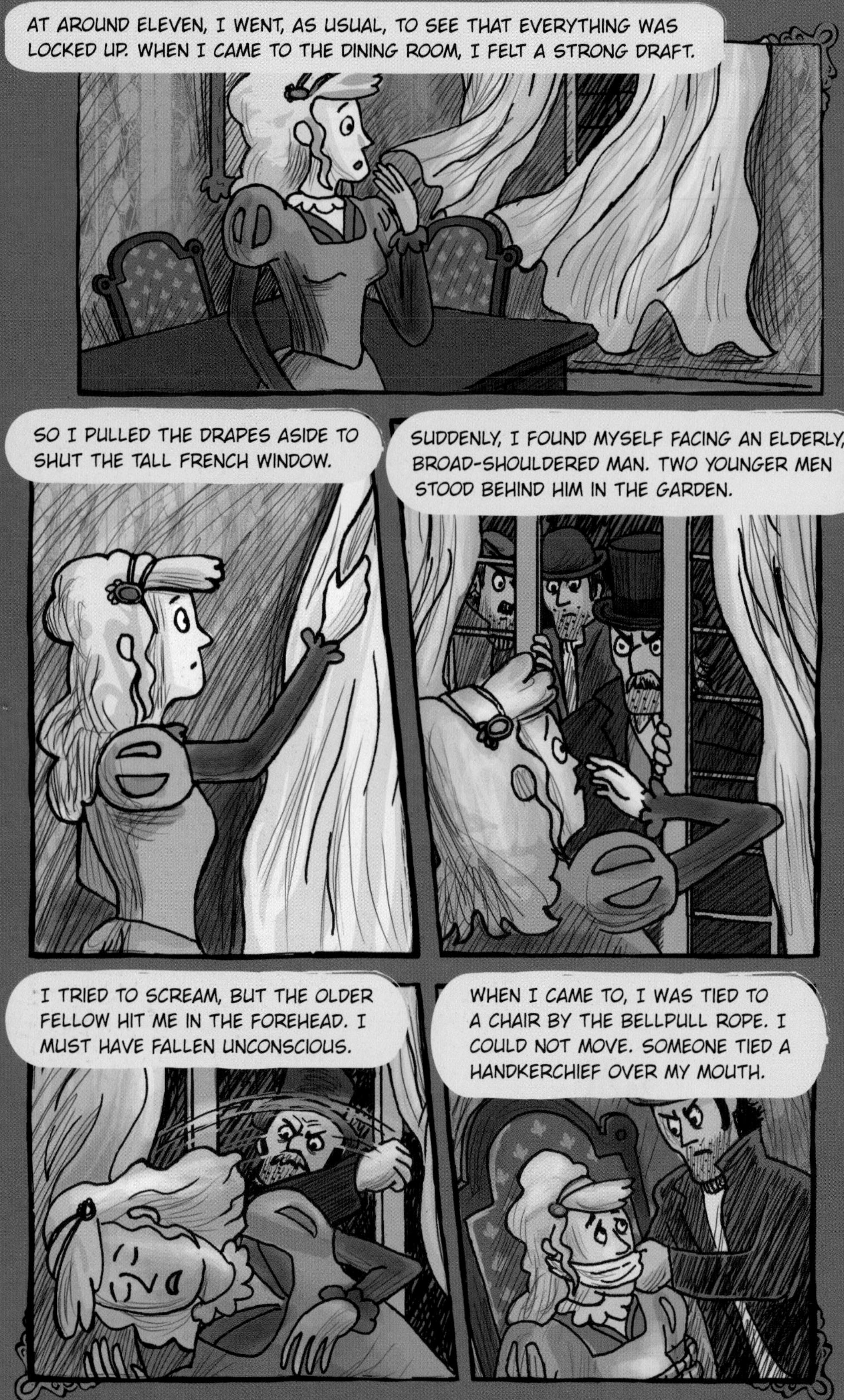
AT AROUND ELEVEN, I WENT, AS USUAL, TO SEE THAT EVERYTHING WAS LOCKED UP. WHEN I CAME TO THE DINING ROOM, I FELT A STRONG DRAFT.
SO I PULLED THE DRAPES ASIDE TO SHUT THE TALL FRENCH WINDOW.
SUDDENLY, I FOUND MYSELF FACING AN ELDERLY, BROAD-SHOULDERED MAN. TWO YOUNGER MEN STOOD BEHIND HIM IN THE GARDEN.
I TRIED TO SCREAM, BUT THE OLDER FELLOW HIT ME IN THE FOREHEAD. I MUST HAVE FALLEN UNCONSCIOUS.
WHEN I CAME TO, I WAS TIED TO A CHAIR BY THE BELLPULL ROPE. I COULD NOT MOVE. SOMEONE TIED A HANDKERCHIEF OVER MY MOUTH.

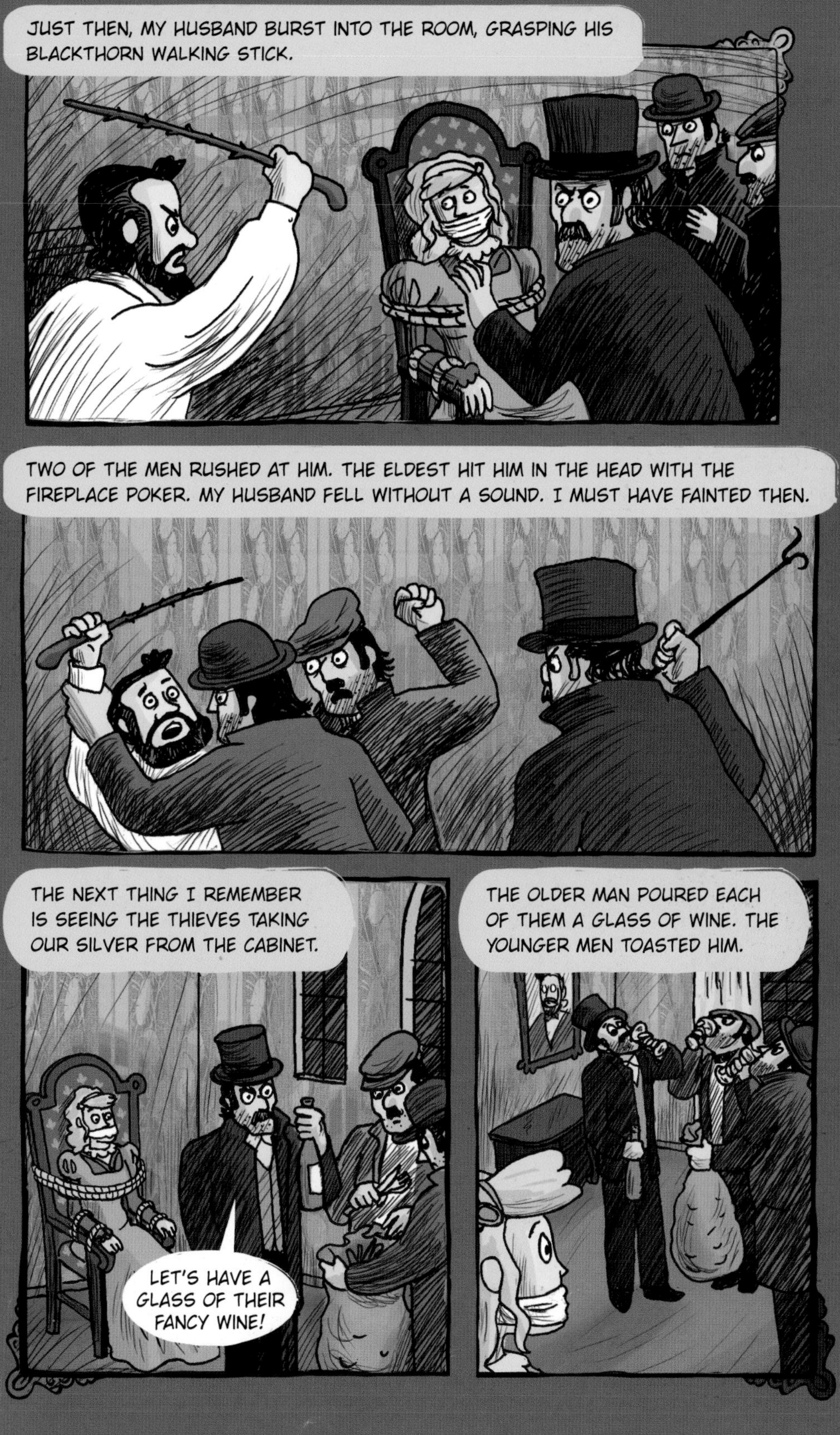
JUST THEN, MY HUSBAND BURST INTO THE ROOM, GRASPING HIS BLACKTHORN WALKING STICK.
TWO OF THE MEN RUSHED AT HIM. THE ELDEST HIT HIM IN THE HEAD WITH THE FIREPLACE POKER. MY HUSBAND FELL WITHOUT A SOUND. I MUST HAVE FAINTED THEN.
THE NEXT THING I REMEMBER IS SEEING THE THIEVES TAKING OUR SILVER FROM THE CABINET.
LET'S HAVE A GLASS OF THEIR FANCY WINE!
THE OLDER MAN POURED EACH OF THEM A GLASS OF WINE. THE YOUNGER MEN TOASTED HIM.

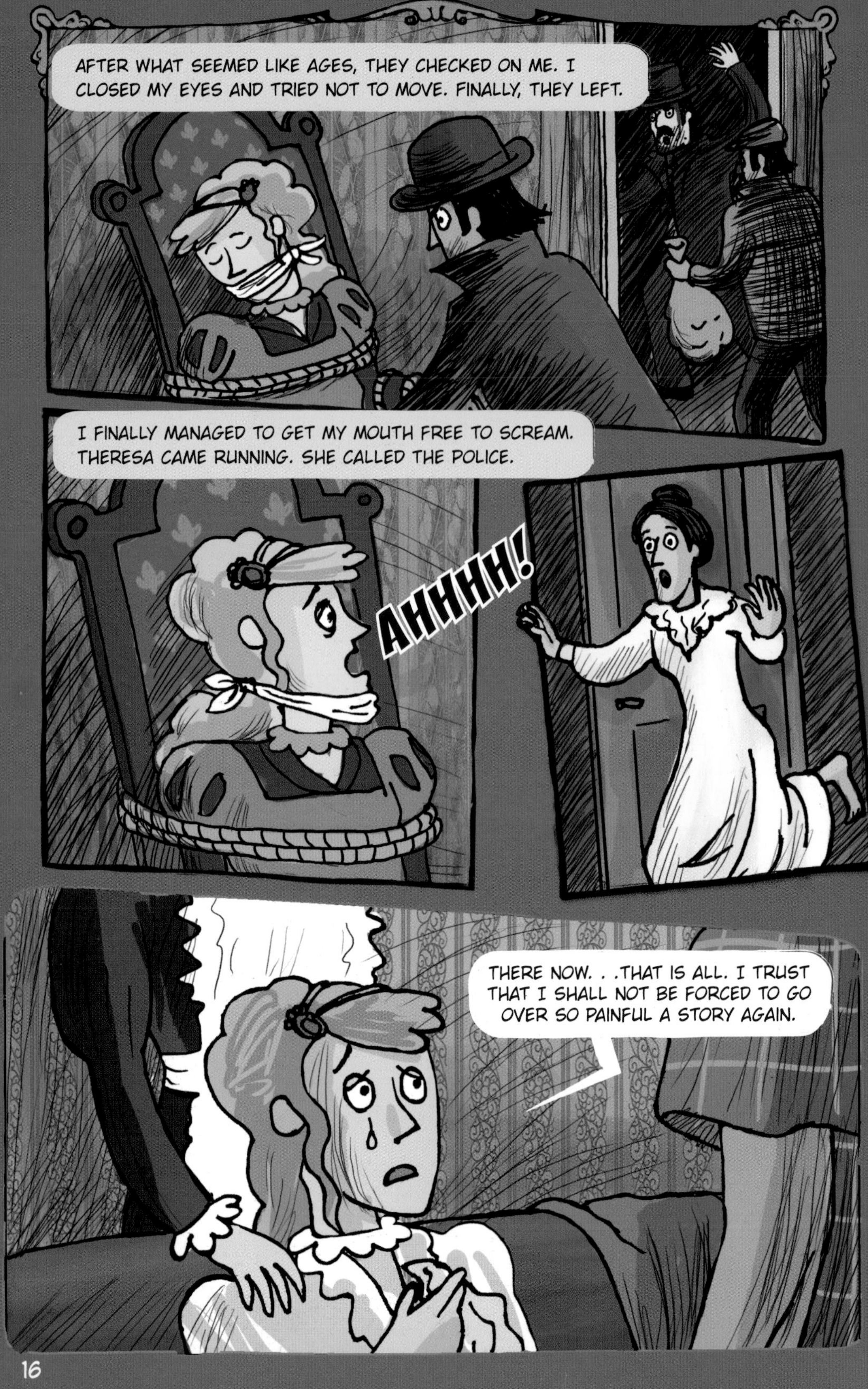
AFTER WHAT SEEMED LIKE AGES, THEY CHECKED ON ME. I CLOSED MY EYES AND TRIED NOT TO MOVE. FINALLY, THEY LEFT.
I FINALLY MANAGED TO GET MY MOUTH FREE TO SCREAM. THERESA CAME RUNNING. SHE CALLED THE POLICE.
AHHHH!
THERE NOW. . .THAT IS ALL. I TRUST THAT I SHALL NOT BE FORCED TO GO OVER SO PAINFUL A STORY AGAIN.

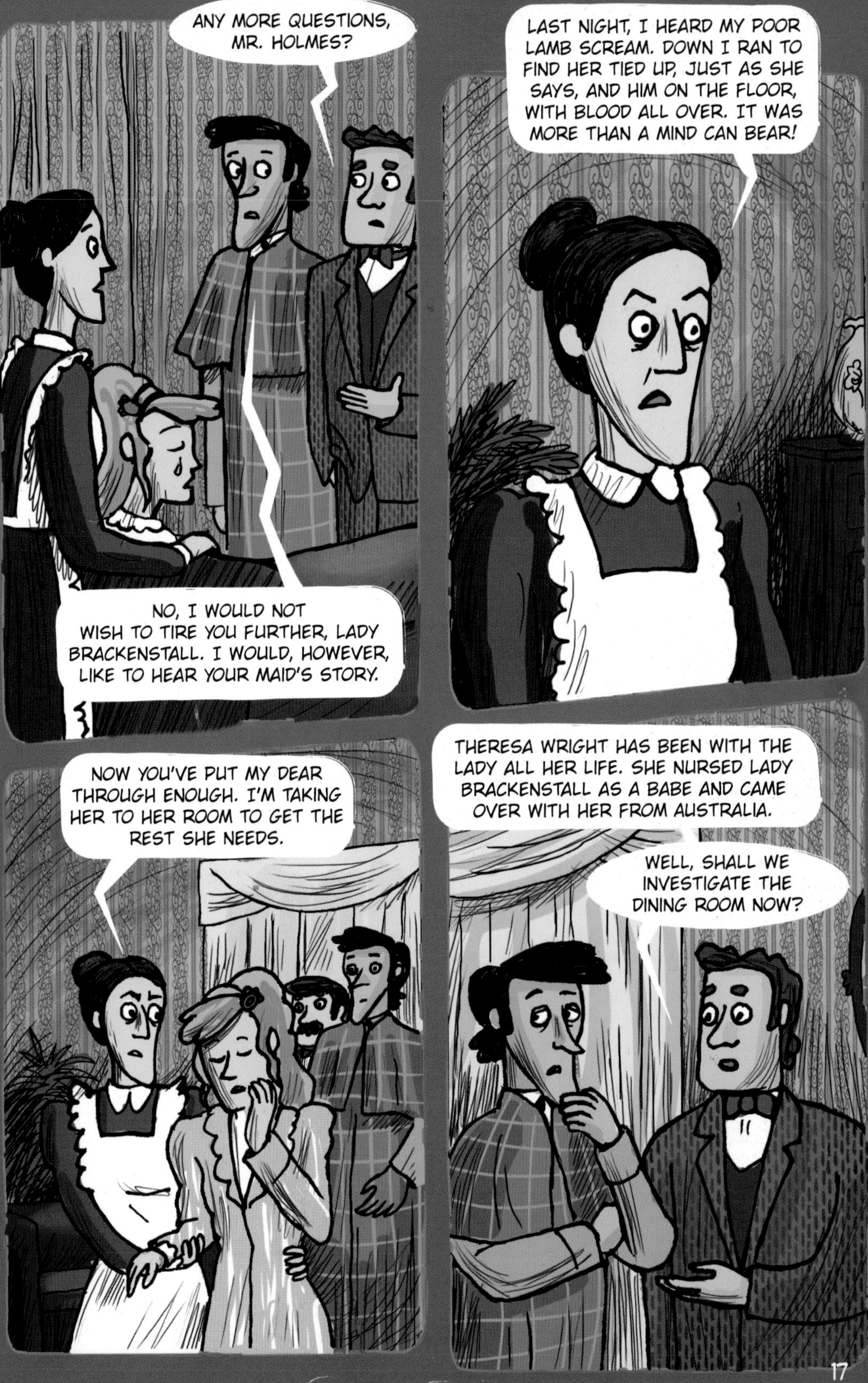
ANY MORE QUESTIONS, MR. HOLMES?
NO, I WOULD NOT WISH TO TIRE YOU FURTHER, LADY BRACKENSTALL. I WOULD, HOWEVER, LIKE TO HEAR YOUR MAID'S STORY.
LAST NIGHT, I HEARD MY POOR LAMB SCREAM. DOWN I RAN TO FIND HER TIED UP, JUST AS SHE SAYS, AND HIM ON THE FLOOR, WITH BLOOD ALL OVER. IT WAS MORE THAN A MIND CAN BEAR!
NOW YOU'VE PUT MY DEAR THROUGH ENOUGH. I'M TAKING HER TO HER ROOM TO GET THE REST SHE NEEDS.
THERESA WRIGHT HAS BEEN WITH THE LADY ALL HER LIFE. SHE NURSED LADY BRACKENSTALL AS A BABE AND CAME OVER WITH HER FROM AUSTRALIA.
WELL, SHALL WE INVESTIGATE THE DINING ROOM NOW?

Holmes did not seem to be listening to Mr. Hopkins. His interest in the case seemed to have passed. He followed Hopkins to the dining room with an air of impatience. But as he entered the room, the strange scene that met him fanned his dying interest.

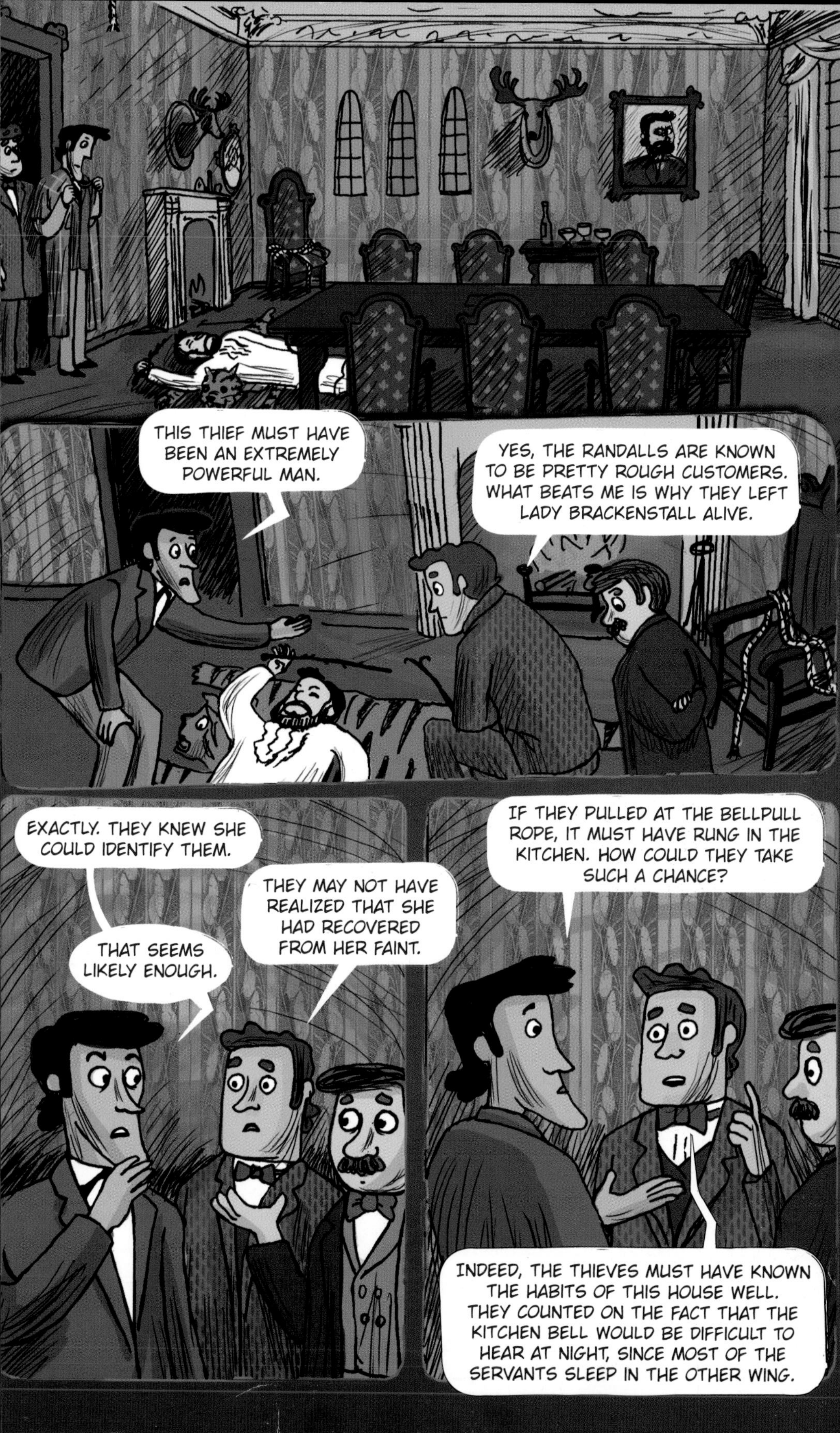
THIS THIEF MUST HAVE BEEN AN EXTREMELY POWERFUL MAN.
YES, THE RANDALLS ARE KNOWN TO BE PRETTY ROUGH CUSTOMERS. WHAT BEATS ME IS WHY THEY LEFT LADY BRACKENSTALL ALIVE.
EXACTLY. THEY KNEW SHE COULD IDENTIFY THEM.
THAT SEEMS LIKELY ENOUGH.
THEY MAY NOT HAVE REALIZED THAT SHE HAD RECOVERED FROM HER FAINT.
IF THEY PULLED AT THE BELLPULL ROPE, IT MUST HAVE RUNG IN THE KITCHEN. HOW COULD THEY TAKE SUCH A CHANCE?
INDEED, THE THIEVES MUST HAVE KNOWN THE HABITS OF THIS HOUSE WELL. THEY COUNTED ON THE FACT THAT THE KITCHEN BELL WOULD BE DIFFICULT TO HEAR AT NIGHT, SINCE MOST OF THE SERVANTS SLEEP IN THE OTHER WING.

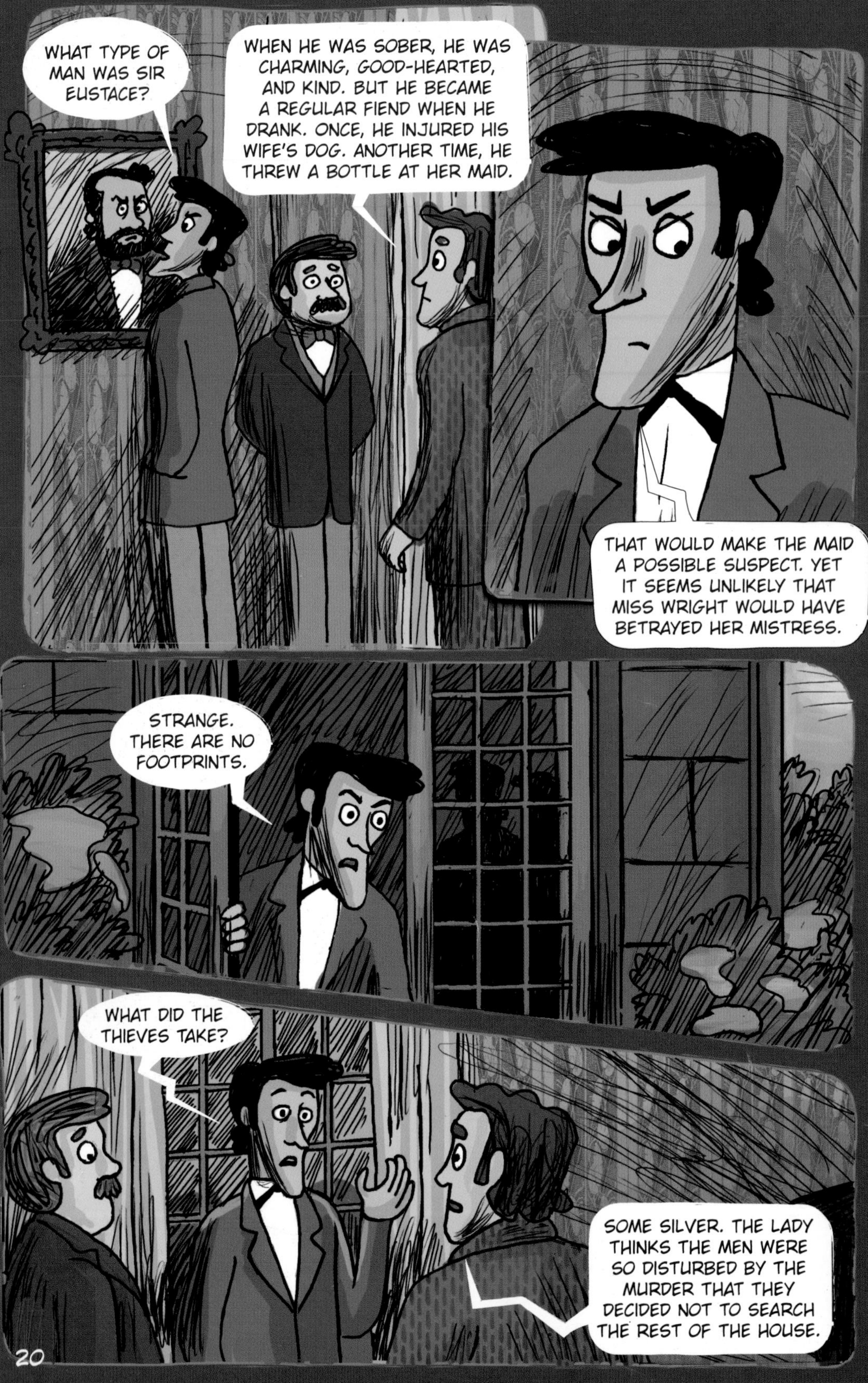
WHAT TYPE OF MAN WAS SIR EUSTACE?
WHEN HE WAS SOBER, HE WAS CHARMING, GOOD-HEARTED, AND KIND. BUT HE BECAME A REGULAR FIEND WHEN HE DRANK. ONCE, HE INJURED HIS WIFE'S DOG. ANOTHER TIME, HE THREW A BOTTLE AT HER MAID.
THAT WOULD MAKE THE MAID A POSSIBLE SUSPECT. YET IT SEEMS UNLIKELY THAT MISS WRIGHT WOULD HAVE BETRAYED HER MISTRESS.
STRANGE. THERE ARE NO FOOTPRINTS.
WHAT DID THE THIEVES TAKE?
SOME SILVER. THE LADY THINKS THE MEN WERE SO DISTURBED BY THE MURDER THAT THEY DECIDED NOT TO SEARCH THE REST OF THE HOUSE.

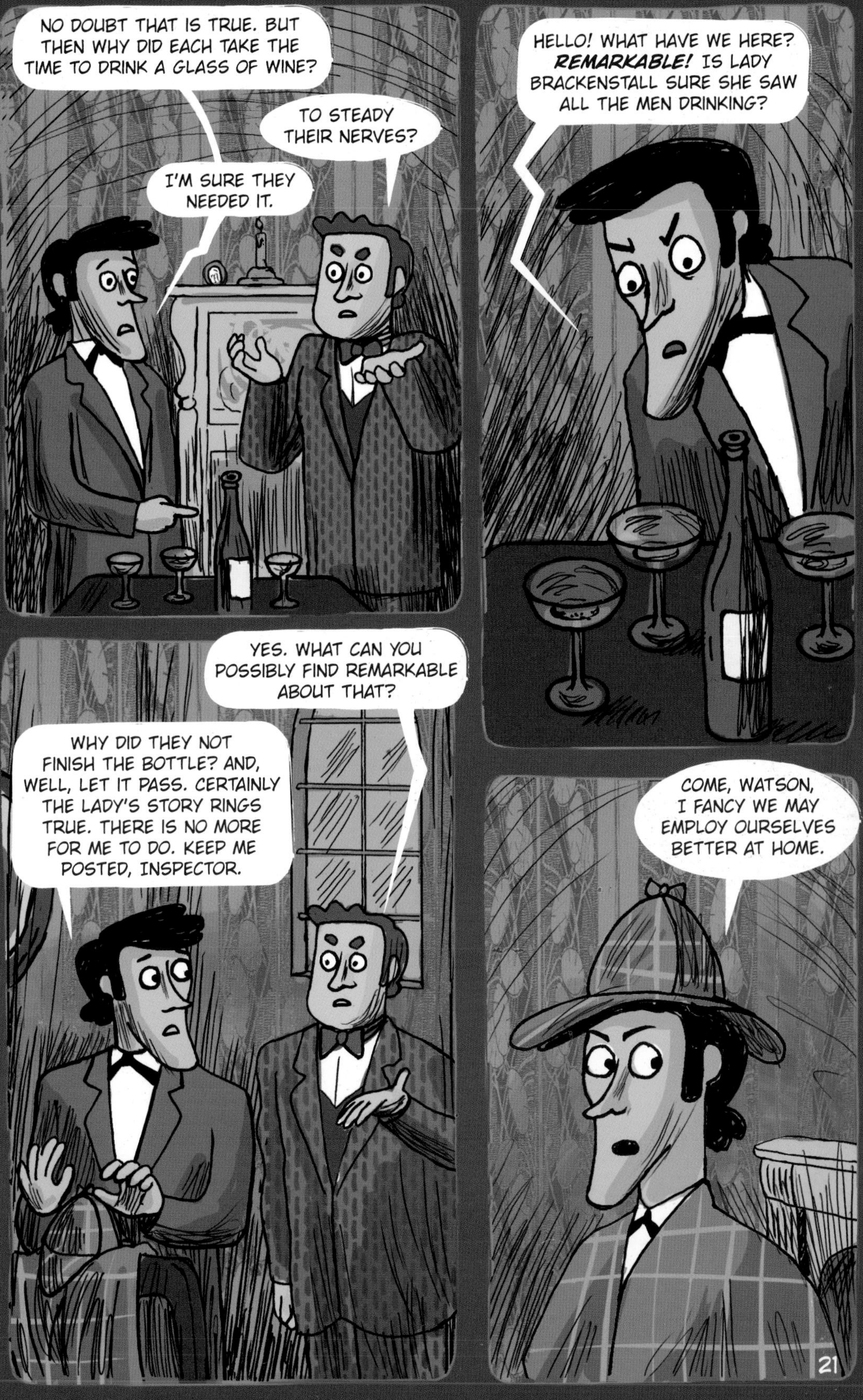
NO DOUBT THAT IS TRUE. BUT THEN WHY DID EACH TAKE THE TIME TO DRINK A GLASS OF WINE?
TO STEADY THEIR NERVES?
I'M SURE THEY NEEDED IT.
HELLO! WHAT HAVE WE HERE? ***REMARKABLE!*** IS LADY BRACKENSTALL SURE SHE SAW ALL THE MEN DRINKING?
YES. WHAT CAN YOU POSSIBLY FIND REMARKABLE ABOUT THAT?
WHY DID THEY NOT FINISH THE BOTTLE? AND, WELL, LET IT PASS. CERTAINLY THE LADY'S STORY RINGS TRUE. THERE IS NO MORE FOR ME TO DO. KEEP ME POSTED, INSPECTOR.
COME, WATSON, I FANCY WE MAY EMPLOY OURSELVES BETTER AT HOME.

During our return journey, I could see that Holmes was still puzzled by certain matters. He would throw off his doubts for a moment, but then his knitted brows would show that the doubts had returned. Just as our train came to one of the stations near London, Holmes sprang onto the platform, and he pulled me with him. Puzzled, I watched as our train pulled away.

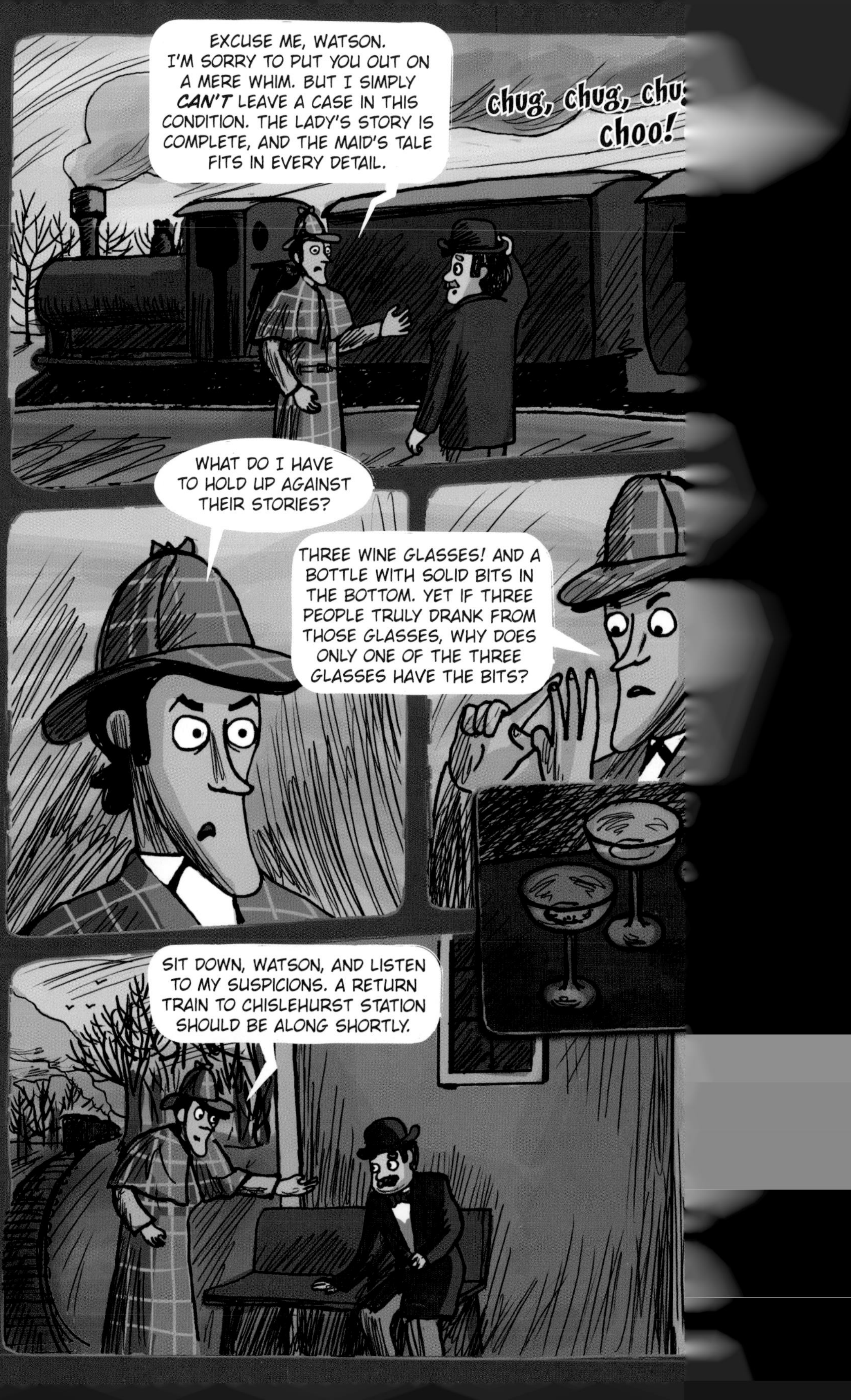
EXCUSE ME, WATSON. I'M SORRY TO PUT YOU OUT ON A MERE WHIM. BUT I SIMPLY CAN'T LEAVE A CASE IN THIS CONDITION. THE LADY'S STORY IS COMPLETE, AND THE MAID'S TALE FITS IN EVERY DETAIL.
chug, chug, chu
choo!
WHAT DO I HAVE TO HOLD UP AGAINST THEIR STORIES?
THREE WINE GLASSES! AND A BOTTLE WITH SOLID BITS IN THE BOTTOM. YET IF THREE PEOPLE TRULY DRANK FROM THOSE GLASSES, WHY DOES ONLY ONE OF THE THREE GLASSES HAVE THE BITS?
SIT DOWN, WATSON, AND LISTEN TO MY SUSPICIONS. A RETURN TRAIN TO CHISLEHURST STATION SHOULD BE ALONG SHORTLY.

The household at the Abbey Grange was much surprised at our return. Inspector Hopkins had left to send his report to Scotland Yard. So Holmes took over the dining room. He locked the door and devoted himself to a thorough two-hour-long investigation. I set myself in a corner and watched his incredible investigation as if I were a student and he, the professor.

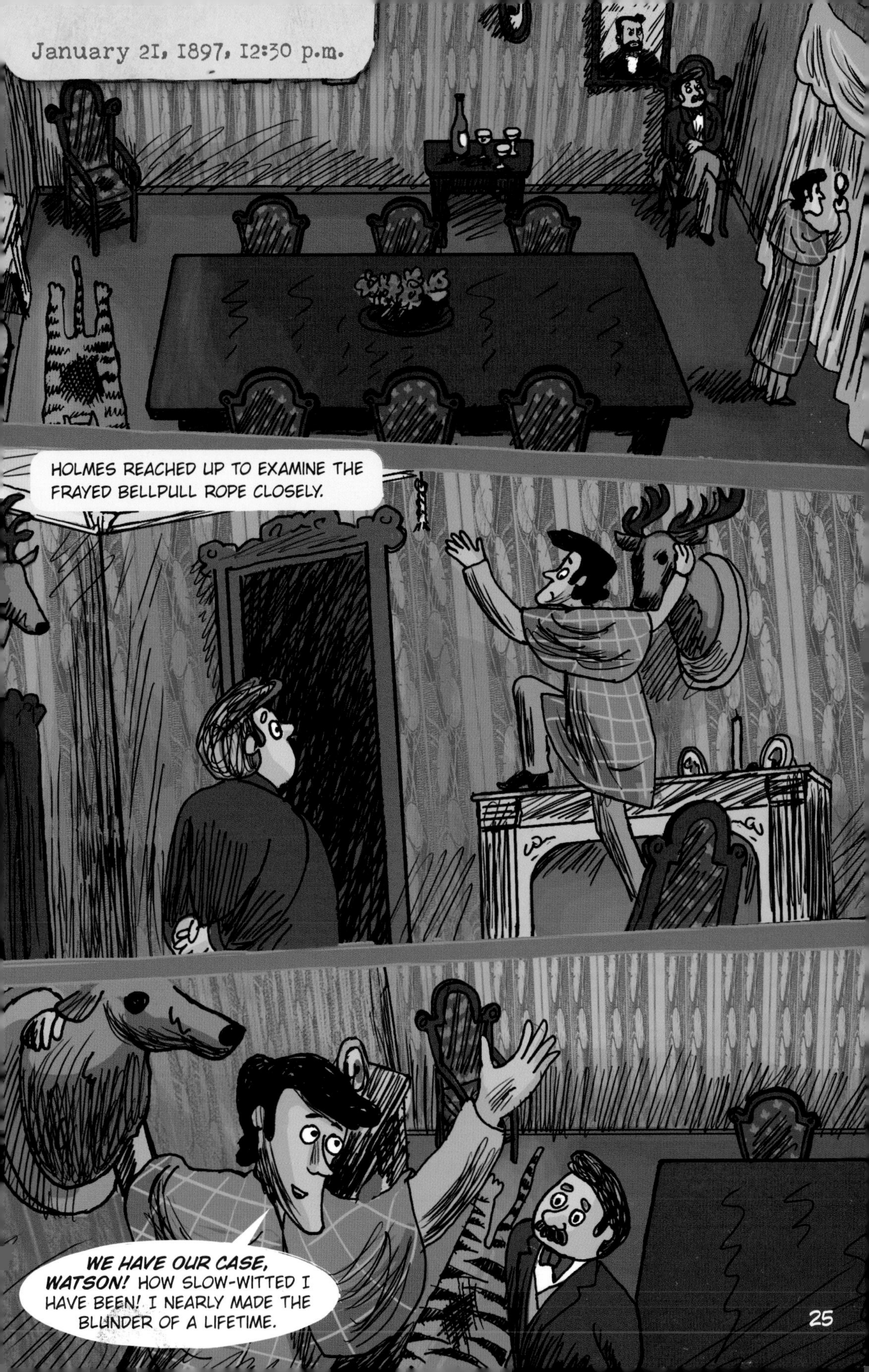
January 21, 1897, 12:30 p.m.
HOLMES REACHED UP TO EXAMINE THE FRAYED BELLPULL ROPE CLOSELY.
WE HAVE OUR CASE, WATSON! HOW SLOW-WITTED I HAVE BEEN! I NEARLY MADE THE BLUNDER OF A LIFETIME.

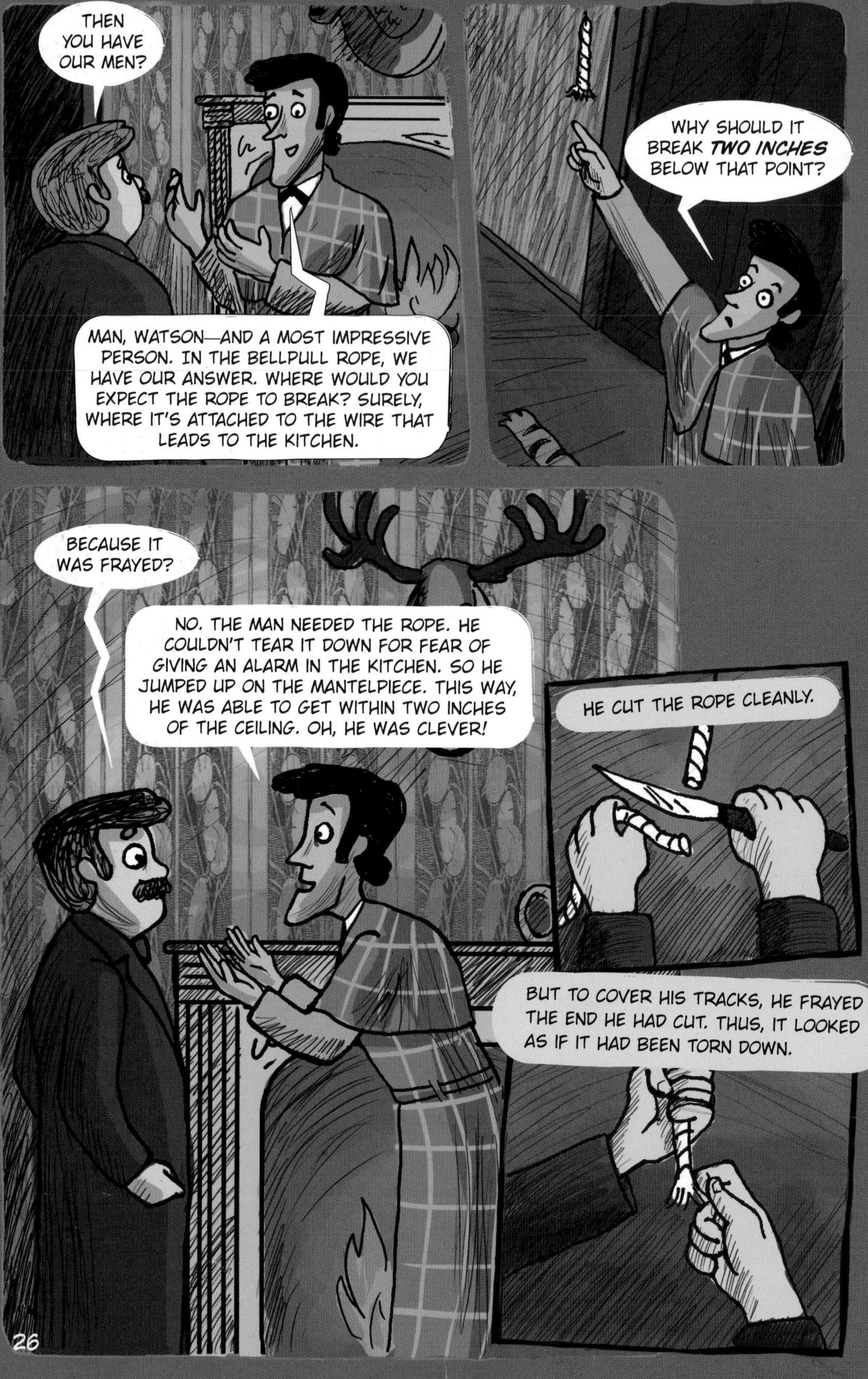
THEN YOU HAVE OUR MEN?
MAN, WATSON—AND A MOST IMPRESSIVE PERSON. IN THE BELLPULL ROPE, WE HAVE OUR ANSWER. WHERE WOULD YOU EXPECT THE ROPE TO BREAK? SURELY, WHERE IT'S ATTACHED TO THE WIRE THAT LEADS TO THE KITCHEN.
WHY SHOULD IT BREAK **TWO INCHES** BELOW THAT POINT?
BECAUSE IT WAS FRAYED?
NO. THE MAN NEEDED THE ROPE. HE COULDN'T TEAR IT DOWN FOR FEAR OF GIVING AN ALARM IN THE KITCHEN. SO HE JUMPED UP ON THE MANTELPIECE. THIS WAY, HE WAS ABLE TO GET WITHIN TWO INCHES OF THE CEILING. OH, HE WAS CLEVER!
HE CUT THE ROPE CLEANLY.
BUT TO COVER HIS TRACKS, HE FRAYED THE END HE HAD CUT. THUS, IT LOOKED AS IF IT HAD BEEN TORN DOWN.

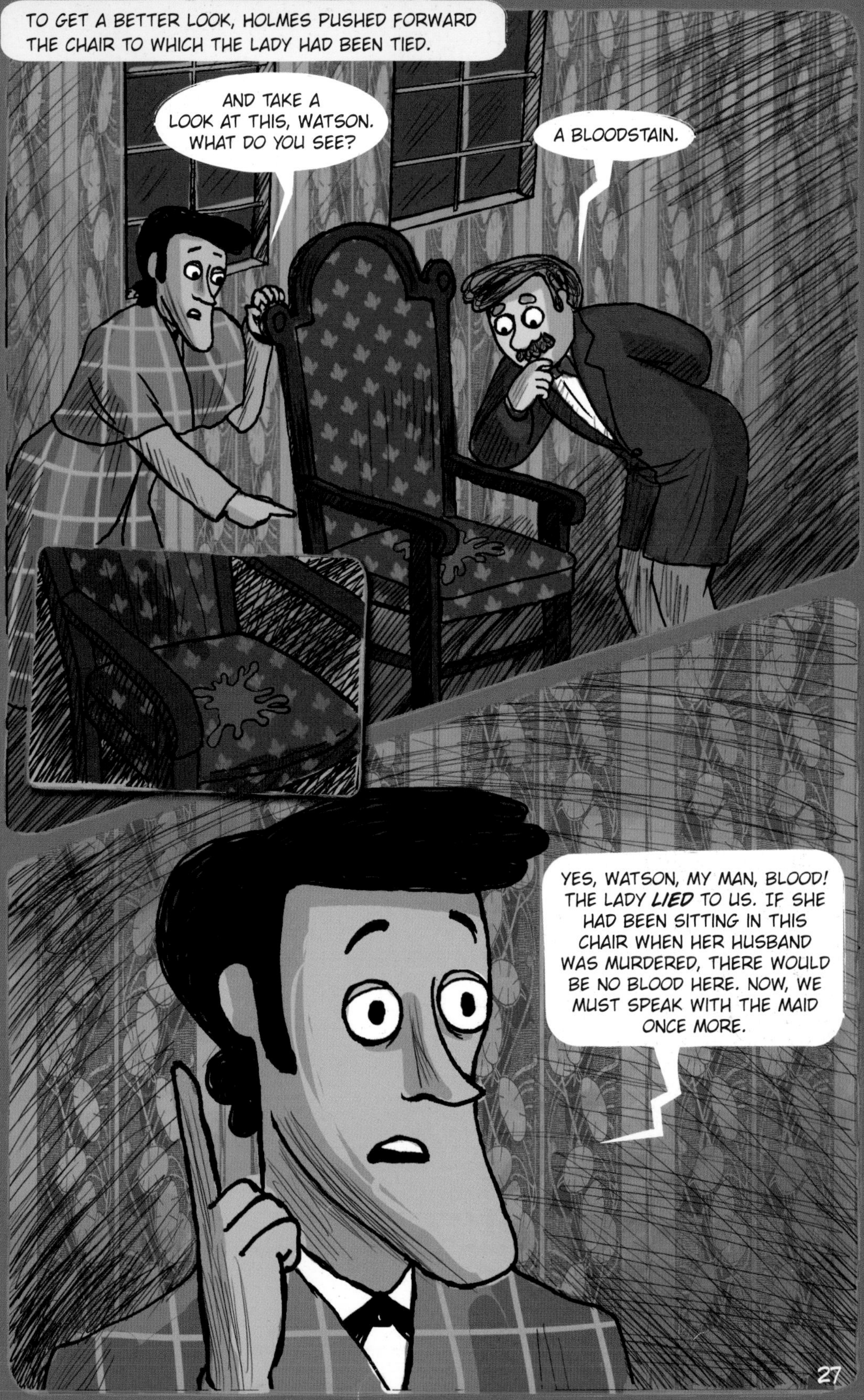

TO GET A BETTER LOOK, HOLMES PUSHED FORWARD THE CHAIR TO WHICH THE LADY HAD BEEN TIED.
AND TAKE A LOOK AT THIS, WATSON. WHAT DO YOU SEE?
A BLOODSTAIN.
YES, WATSON, MY MAN, BLOOD! THE LADY ***LIED*** TO US. IF SHE HAD BEEN SITTING IN THIS CHAIR WHEN HER HUSBAND WAS MURDERED, THERE WOULD BE NO BLOOD HERE. NOW, WE MUST SPEAK WITH THE MAID ONCE MORE.

When Holmes approached Theresa Wright, she watched him as if he were a tiger ready to pounce. But eventually, my friend's pleasant manner made her relax and speak. She did not even try to conceal her hatred for her late employer.

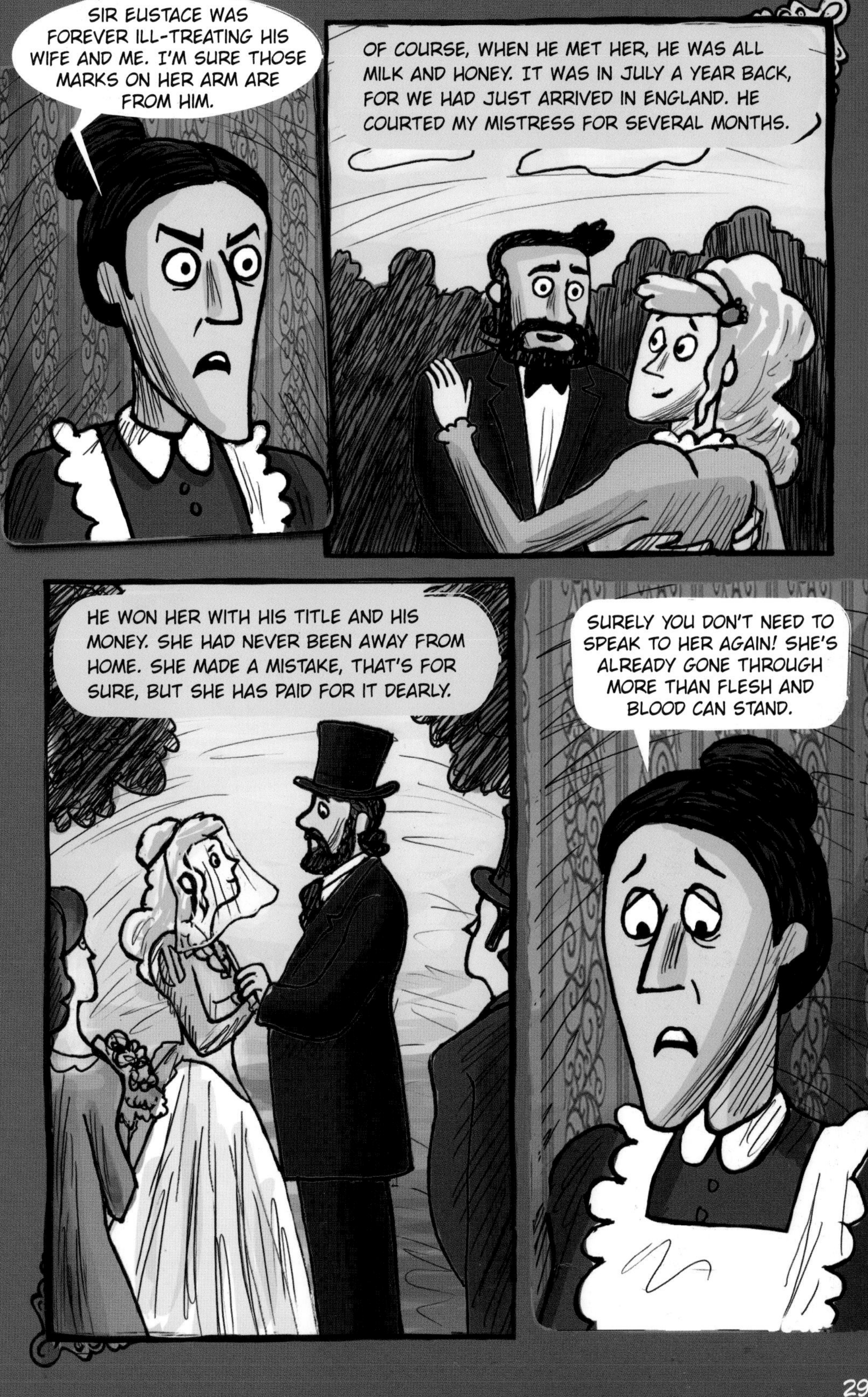
SIR EUSTACE WAS FOREVER ILL-TREATING HIS WIFE AND ME. I'M SURE THOSE MARKS ON HER ARM ARE FROM HIM.
OF COURSE, WHEN HE MET HER, HE WAS ALL MILK AND HONEY. IT WAS IN JULY A YEAR BACK, FOR WE HAD JUST ARRIVED IN ENGLAND. HE COURTED MY MISTRESS FOR SEVERAL MONTHS.
HE WON HER WITH HIS TITLE AND HIS MONEY. SHE HAD NEVER BEEN AWAY FROM HOME. SHE MADE A MISTAKE, THAT'S FOR SURE, BUT SHE HAS PAID FOR IT DEARLY.
SURELY YOU DON'T NEED TO SPEAK TO HER AGAIN! SHE'S ALREADY GONE THROUGH MORE THAN FLESH AND BLOOD CAN STAND.

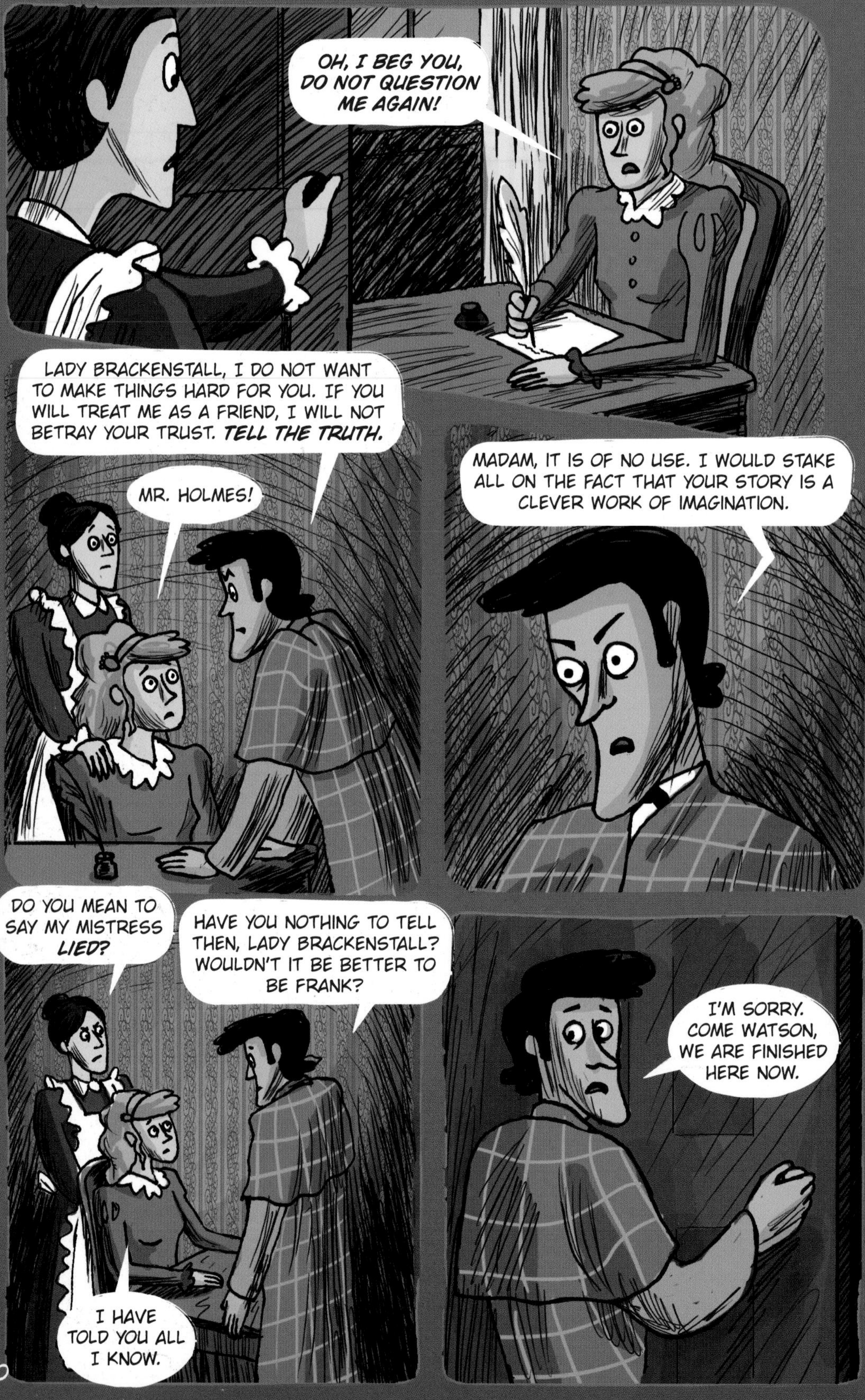
OH, I BEG YOU, DO NOT QUESTION ME AGAIN!
LADY BRACKENSTALL, I DO NOT WANT TO MAKE THINGS HARD FOR YOU. IF YOU WILL TREAT ME AS A FRIEND, I WILL NOT BETRAY YOUR TRUST. TELL THE TRUTH.
MR. HOLMES!
MADAM, IT IS OF NO USE. I WOULD STAKE ALL ON THE FACT THAT YOUR STORY IS A CLEVER WORK OF IMAGINATION.
DO YOU MEAN TO SAY MY MISTRESS LIED?
HAVE YOU NOTHING TO TELL THEN, LADY BRACKENSTALL? WOULDN'T IT BE BETTER TO BE FRANK?
I HAVE TOLD YOU ALL I KNOW.
I'M SORRY. COME WATSON, WE ARE FINISHED HERE NOW.

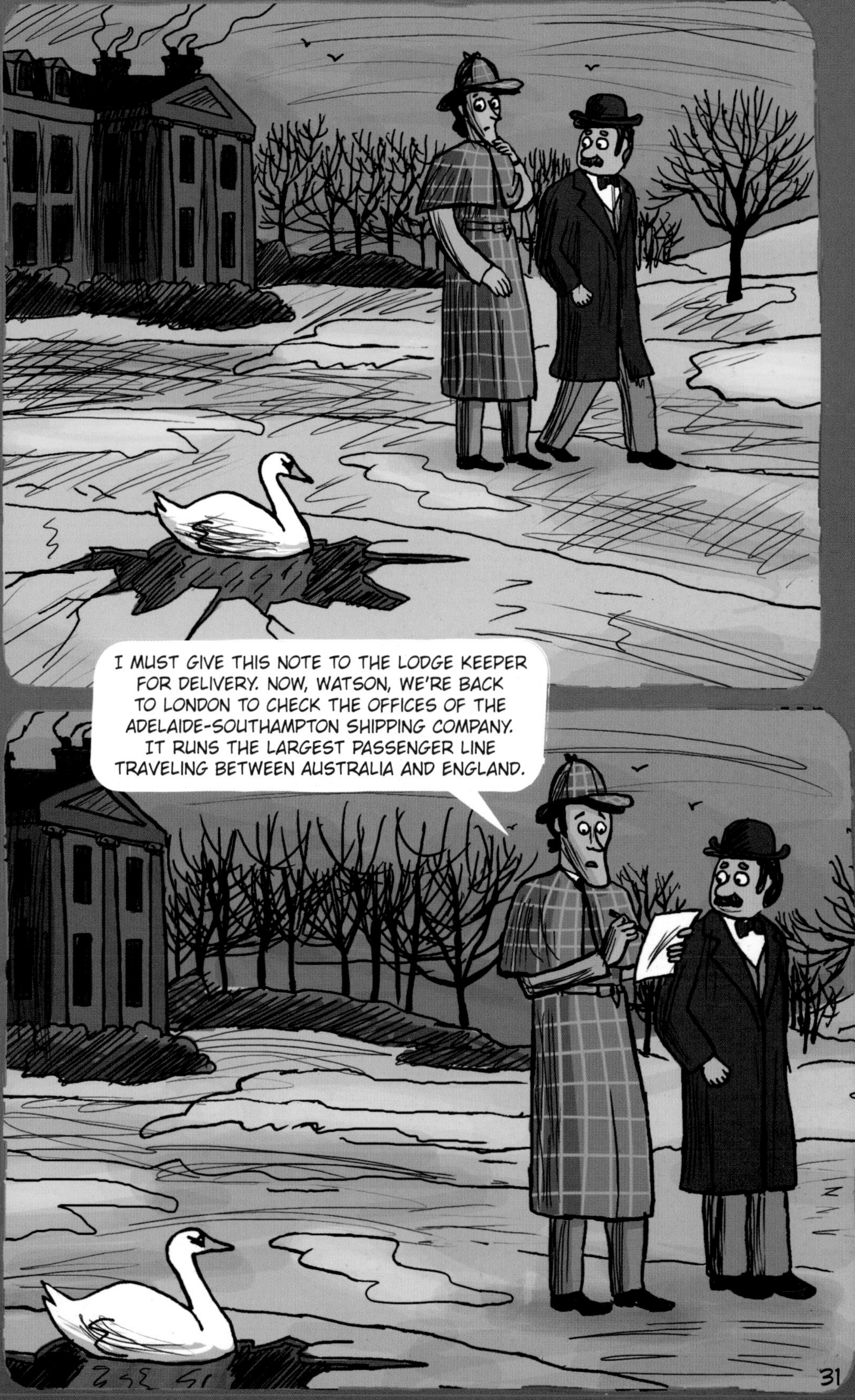
I MUST GIVE THIS NOTE TO THE LODGE KEEPER FOR DELIVERY. NOW, WATSON, WE'RE BACK TO LONDON TO CHECK THE OFFICES OF THE ADELAIDE-SOUTHAMPTON SHIPPING COMPANY. IT RUNS THE LARGEST PASSENGER LINE TRAVELING BETWEEN AUSTRALIA AND ENGLAND.

When Holmes's card was brought in to the manager of the shipping company, we received instant attention. Holmes asked to see the passenger lists from June and July of 1895. The lists showed what he was looking for, but I had to ponder where this bit of information was taking him.

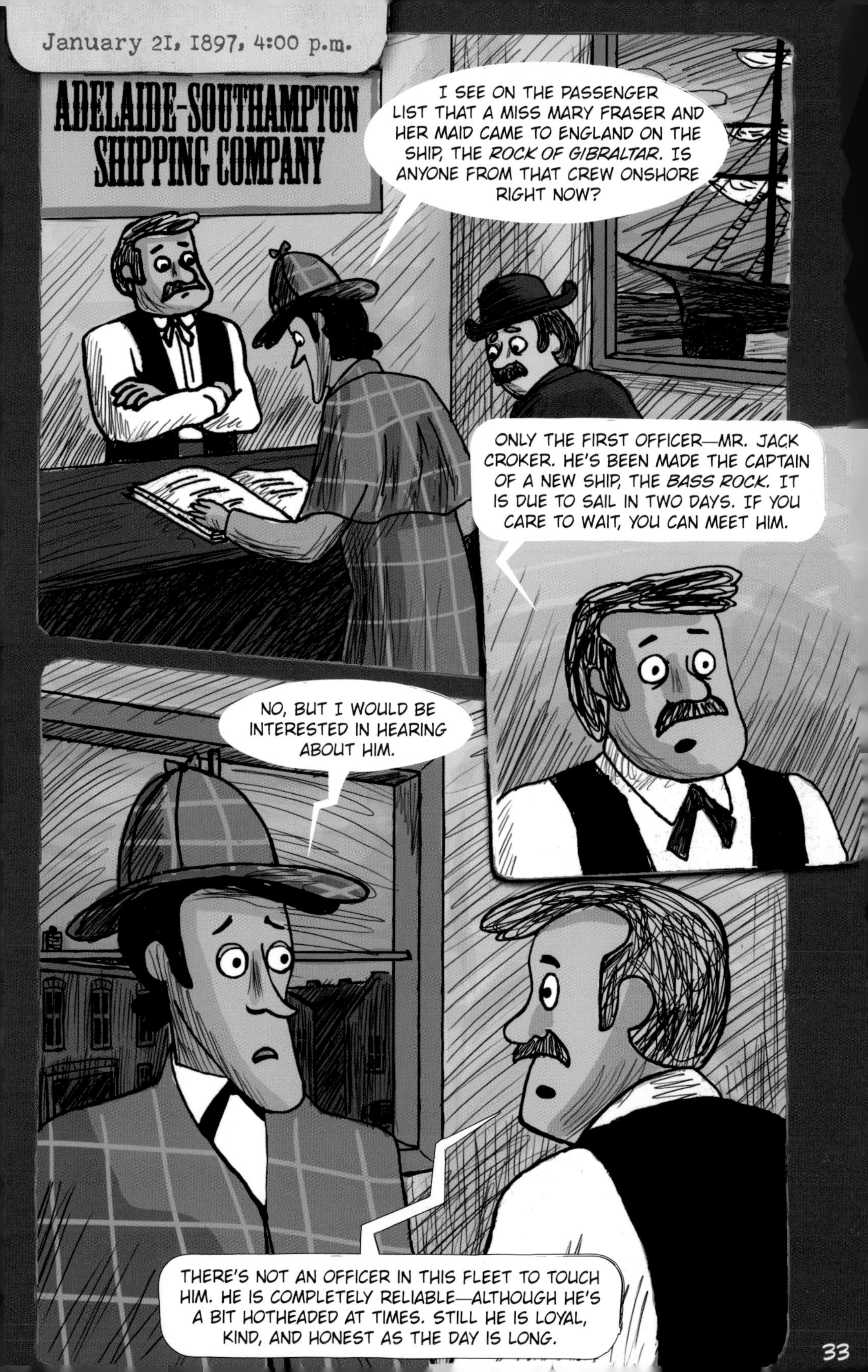
January 21, 1897, 4:00 p.m.
ADELAIDE-SOUTHAMPTON SHIPPING COMPANY
I SEE ON THE PASSENGER LIST THAT A MISS MARY FRASER AND HER MAID CAME TO ENGLAND ON THE SHIP, THE *ROCK OF GIBRALTAR*. IS ANYONE FROM THAT CREW ONSHORE RIGHT NOW?
ONLY THE FIRST OFFICER—MR. JACK CROKER. HE'S BEEN MADE THE CAPTAIN OF A NEW SHIP, THE *BASS ROCK*. IT IS DUE TO SAIL IN TWO DAYS. IF YOU CARE TO WAIT, YOU CAN MEET HIM.
NO, BUT I WOULD BE INTERESTED IN HEARING ABOUT HIM.
THERE'S NOT AN OFFICER IN THIS FLEET TO TOUCH HIM. HE IS COMPLETELY RELIABLE—ALTHOUGH HE'S A BIT HOTHEADED AT TIMES. STILL HE IS LOYAL, KIND, AND HONEST AS THE DAY IS LONG.

Upon leaving the shipping office, we drove to Scotland Yard. But Holmes did not enter. He sat in the cab, lost in thought. I could contain my curiosity no longer and wanted to ask if he had found his man. Instead, I held my tongue. I asked a more routine question.

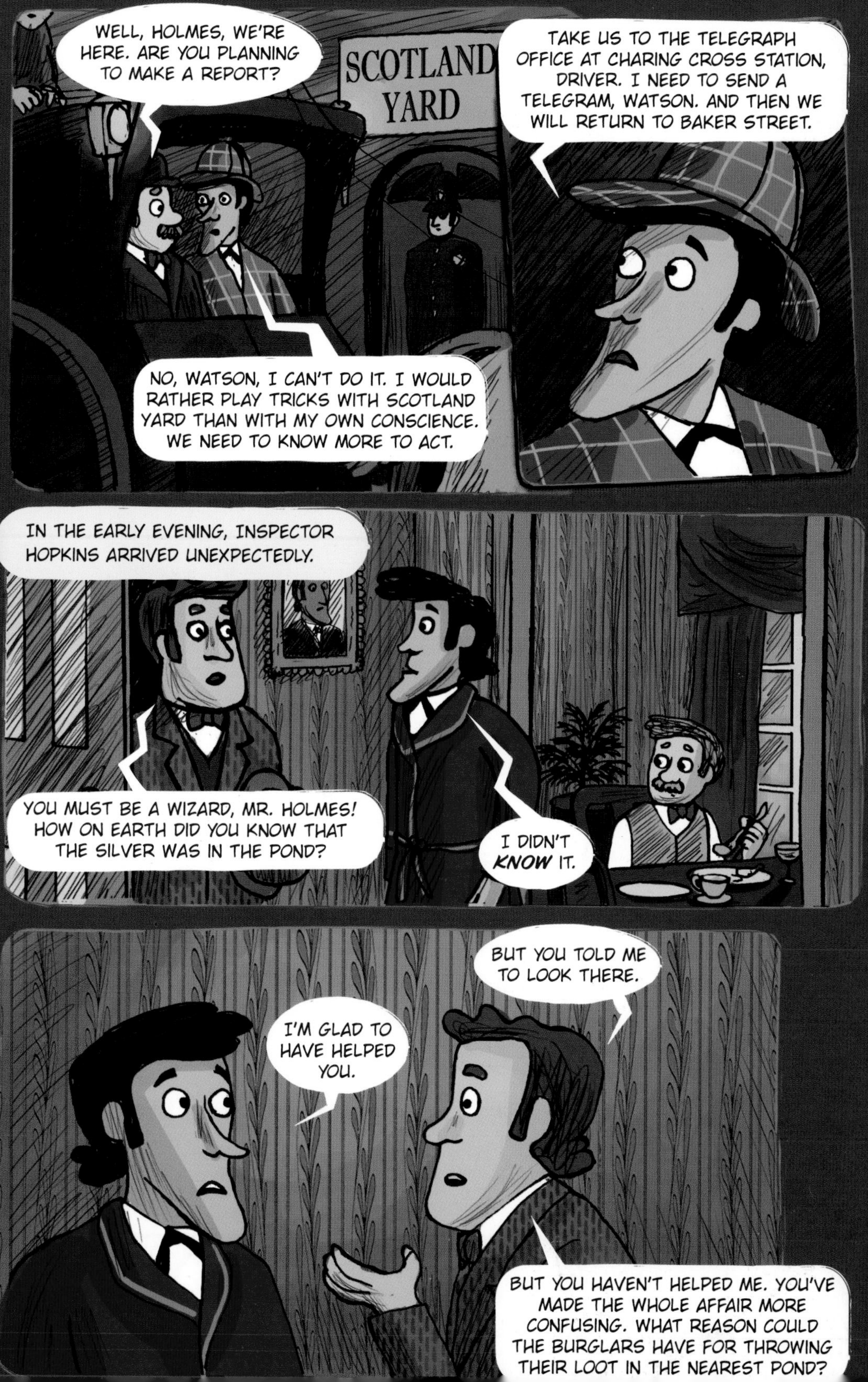
WELL, HOLMES, WE'RE HERE. ARE YOU PLANNING TO MAKE A REPORT?
SCOTLAND YARD
NO, WATSON, I CAN'T DO IT. I WOULD RATHER PLAY TRICKS WITH SCOTLAND YARD THAN WITH MY OWN CONSCIENCE. WE NEED TO KNOW MORE TO ACT.
TAKE US TO THE TELEGRAPH OFFICE AT CHARING CROSS STATION, DRIVER. I NEED TO SEND A TELEGRAM, WATSON. AND THEN WE WILL RETURN TO BAKER STREET.
IN THE EARLY EVENING, INSPECTOR HOPKINS ARRIVED UNEXPECTEDLY.
YOU MUST BE A WIZARD, MR. HOLMES! HOW ON EARTH DID YOU KNOW THAT THE SILVER WAS IN THE POND?
I DIDN'T ***KNOW*** IT.
BUT YOU TOLD ME TO LOOK THERE.
I'M GLAD TO HAVE HELPED YOU.
BUT YOU HAVEN'T HELPED ME. YOU'VE MADE THE WHOLE AFFAIR MORE CONFUSING. WHAT REASON COULD THE BURGLARS HAVE FOR THROWING THEIR LOOT IN THE NEAREST POND?

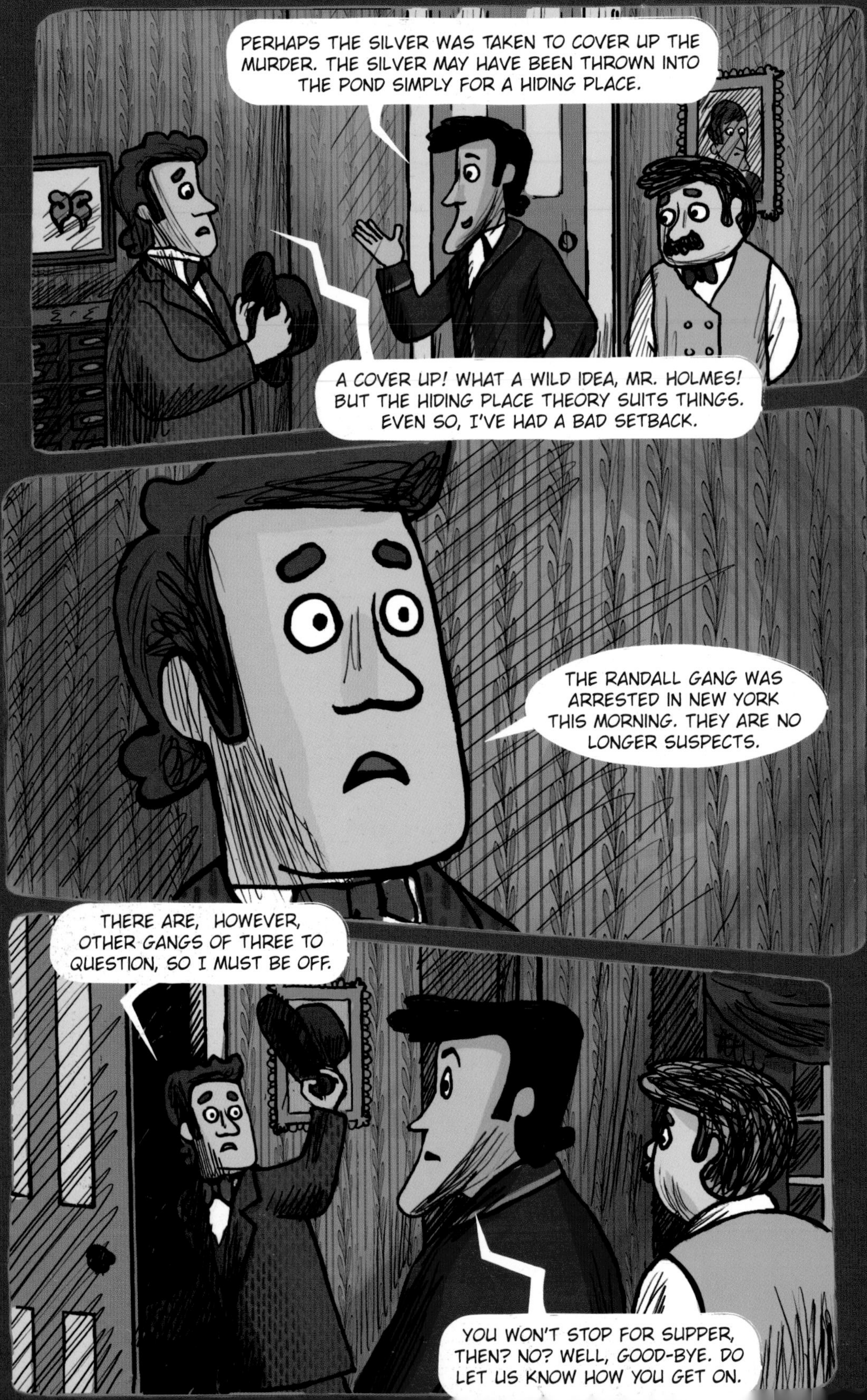
PERHAPS THE SILVER WAS TAKEN TO COVER UP THE MURDER. THE SILVER MAY HAVE BEEN THROWN INTO THE POND SIMPLY FOR A HIDING PLACE.
A COVER UP! WHAT A WILD IDEA, MR. HOLMES! BUT THE HIDING PLACE THEORY SUITS THINGS. EVEN SO, I'VE HAD A BAD SETBACK.
THE RANDALL GANG WAS ARRESTED IN NEW YORK THIS MORNING. THEY ARE NO LONGER SUSPECTS.
THERE ARE, HOWEVER, OTHER GANGS OF THREE TO QUESTION, SO I MUST BE OFF.
YOU WON'T STOP FOR SUPPER, THEN? NO? WELL, GOOD-BYE. DO LET US KNOW HOW YOU GET ON.

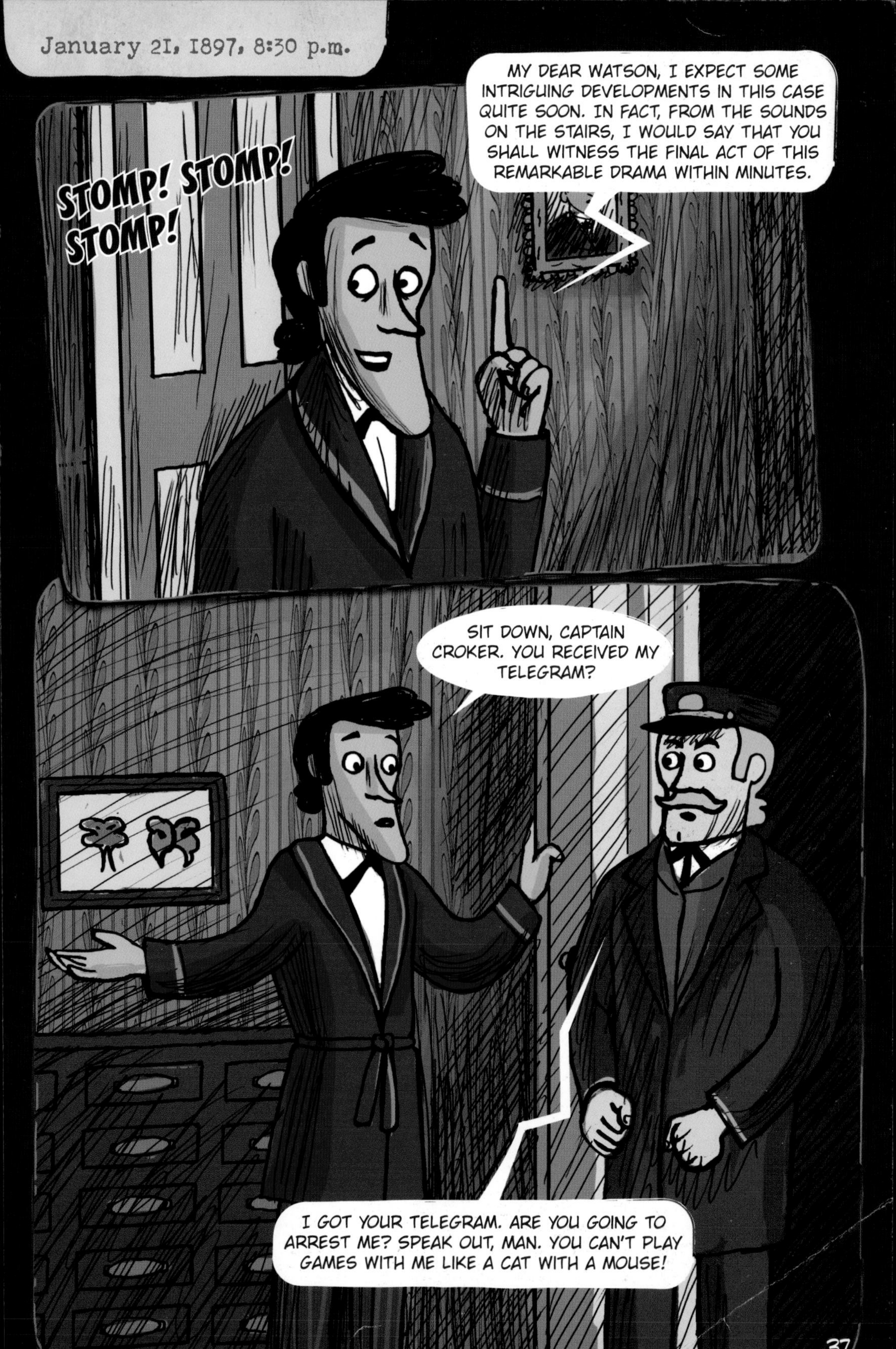
January 21, 1897, 8:30 p.m.
STOMP! STOMP! STOMP!
MY DEAR WATSON, I EXPECT SOME INTRIGUING DEVELOPMENTS IN THIS CASE QUITE SOON. IN FACT, FROM THE SOUNDS ON THE STAIRS, I WOULD SAY THAT YOU SHALL WITNESS THE FINAL ACT OF THIS REMARKABLE DRAMA WITHIN MINUTES.
SIT DOWN, CAPTAIN CROKER. YOU RECEIVED MY TELEGRAM?
I GOT YOUR TELEGRAM. ARE YOU GOING TO ARREST ME? SPEAK OUT, MAN. YOU CAN'T PLAY GAMES WITH ME LIKE A CAT WITH A MOUSE!

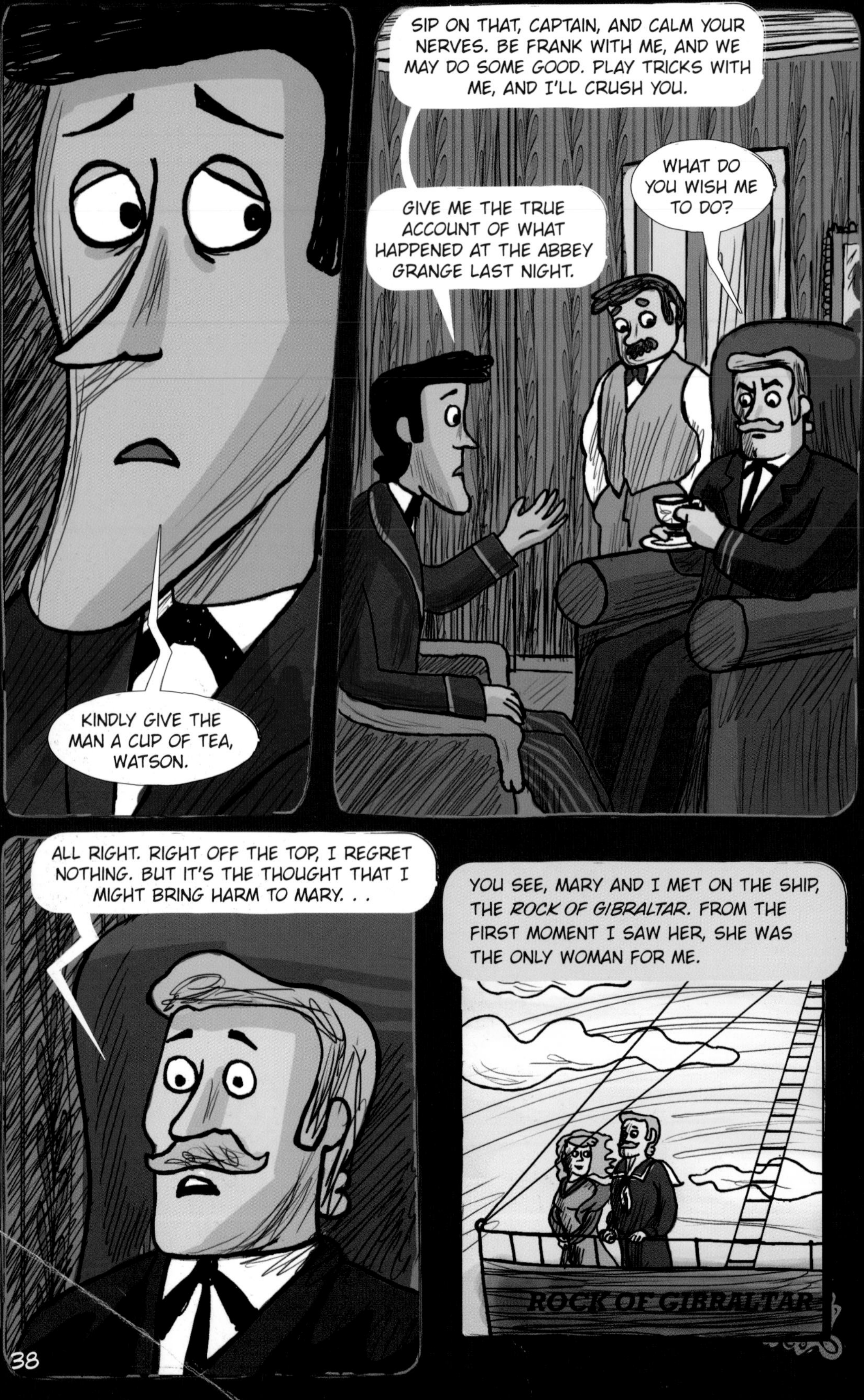
KINDLY GIVE THE MAN A CUP OF TEA, WATSON.
SIP ON THAT, CAPTAIN, AND CALM YOUR NERVES. BE FRANK WITH ME, AND WE MAY DO SOME GOOD. PLAY TRICKS WITH ME, AND I'LL CRUSH YOU.
WHAT DO YOU WISH ME TO DO?
GIVE ME THE TRUE ACCOUNT OF WHAT HAPPENED AT THE ABBEY GRANGE LAST NIGHT.
ALL RIGHT. RIGHT OFF THE TOP, I REGRET NOTHING. BUT IT'S THE THOUGHT THAT I MIGHT BRING HARM TO MARY. . .
YOU SEE, MARY AND I MET ON THE SHIP, THE *ROCK OF GIBRALTAR*. FROM THE FIRST MOMENT I SAW HER, SHE WAS THE ONLY WOMAN FOR ME.
ROCK OF GIBRALTAR

THE NEXT TIME WE DOCKED, I HEARD OF HER MARRIAGE. I WAS HAPPY FOR HER. I KNEW SHE DESERVED MUCH MORE THAN A PENNILESS SAILOR COULD GIVE HER.

THEN ONE DAY, I CAUGHT SIGHT OF HER MAID. THE WOMAN DROVE ME *HALF MAD* WITH HER STORY. THAT DRUNKEN HOUND, SIR EUSTACE—THAT HE SHOULD *DARE* TO RAISE A HAND AGAINST MY MARY!

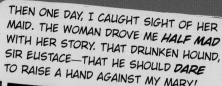

THERESA ARRANGED THAT I COULD MEET MARY ON A FEW OCCASIONS.

THEN MY ORDERS ARRIVED. I SIMPLY HAD TO SEE MARY ONCE MORE. SO LAST NIGHT, I TAPPED AT THE LIBRARY WINDOW. AT FIRST, MARY IGNORED ME.

BUT FINALLY, SHE COULD NOT LEAVE ME OUT IN THE FROSTY NIGHT. SHE HAD ME COME TO THE DINING ROOM, WHERE SHE LET ME IN.

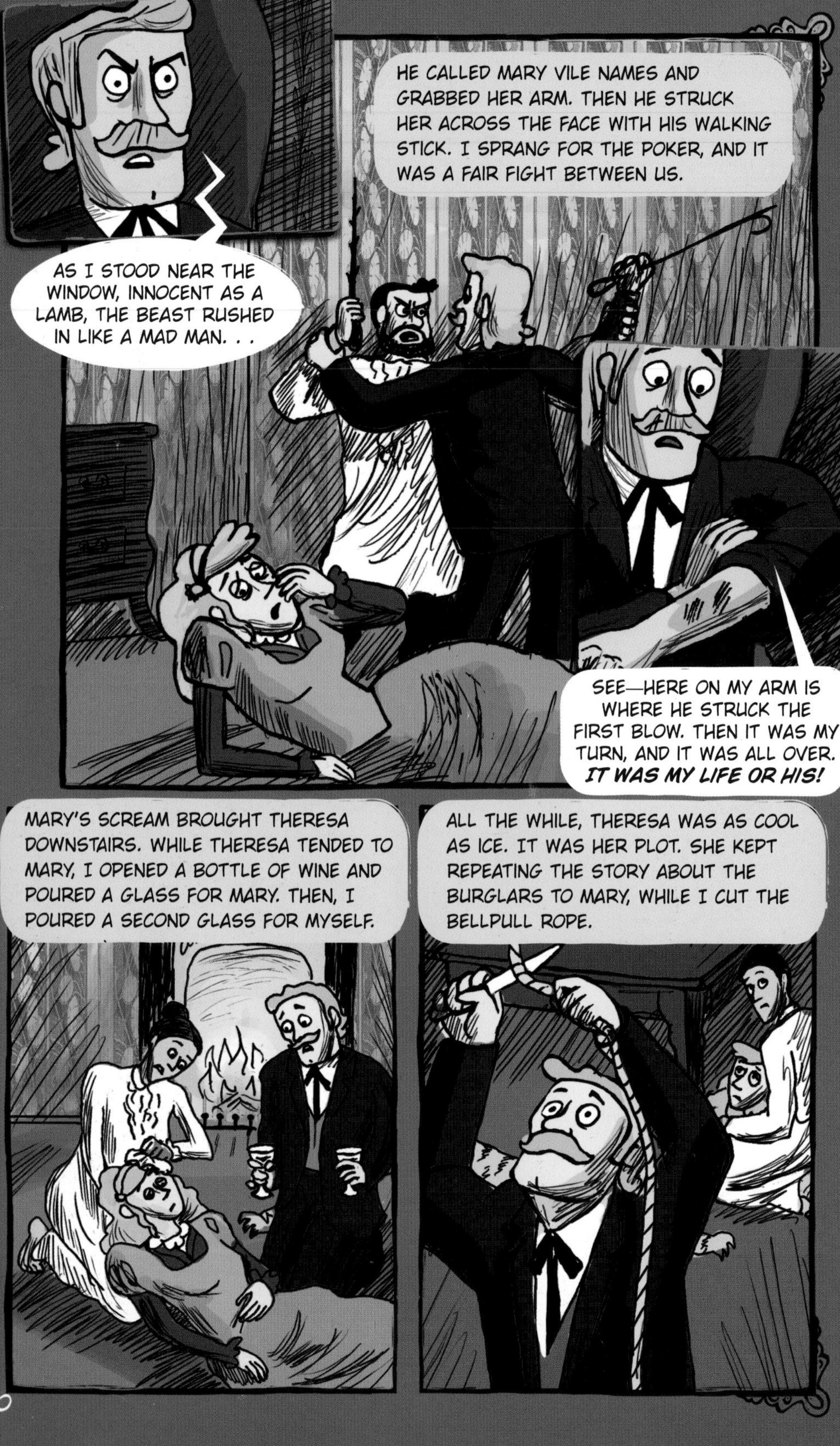

HE CALLED MARY VILE NAMES AND GRABBED HER ARM. THEN HE STRUCK HER ACROSS THE FACE WITH HIS WALKING STICK. I SPRANG FOR THE POKER, AND IT WAS A FAIR FIGHT BETWEEN US.
AS I STOOD NEAR THE WINDOW, INNOCENT AS A LAMB, THE BEAST RUSHED IN LIKE A MAD MAN. . .
SEE—HERE ON MY ARM IS WHERE HE STRUCK THE FIRST BLOW. THEN IT WAS MY TURN, AND IT WAS ALL OVER. ***IT WAS MY LIFE OR HIS!***
MARY'S SCREAM BROUGHT THERESA DOWNSTAIRS. WHILE THERESA TENDED TO MARY, I OPENED A BOTTLE OF WINE AND POURED A GLASS FOR MARY. THEN, I POURED A SECOND GLASS FOR MYSELF.
ALL THE WHILE, THERESA WAS AS COOL AS ICE. IT WAS HER PLOT. SHE KEPT REPEATING THE STORY ABOUT THE BURGLARS TO MARY, WHILE I CUT THE BELLPULL ROPE.

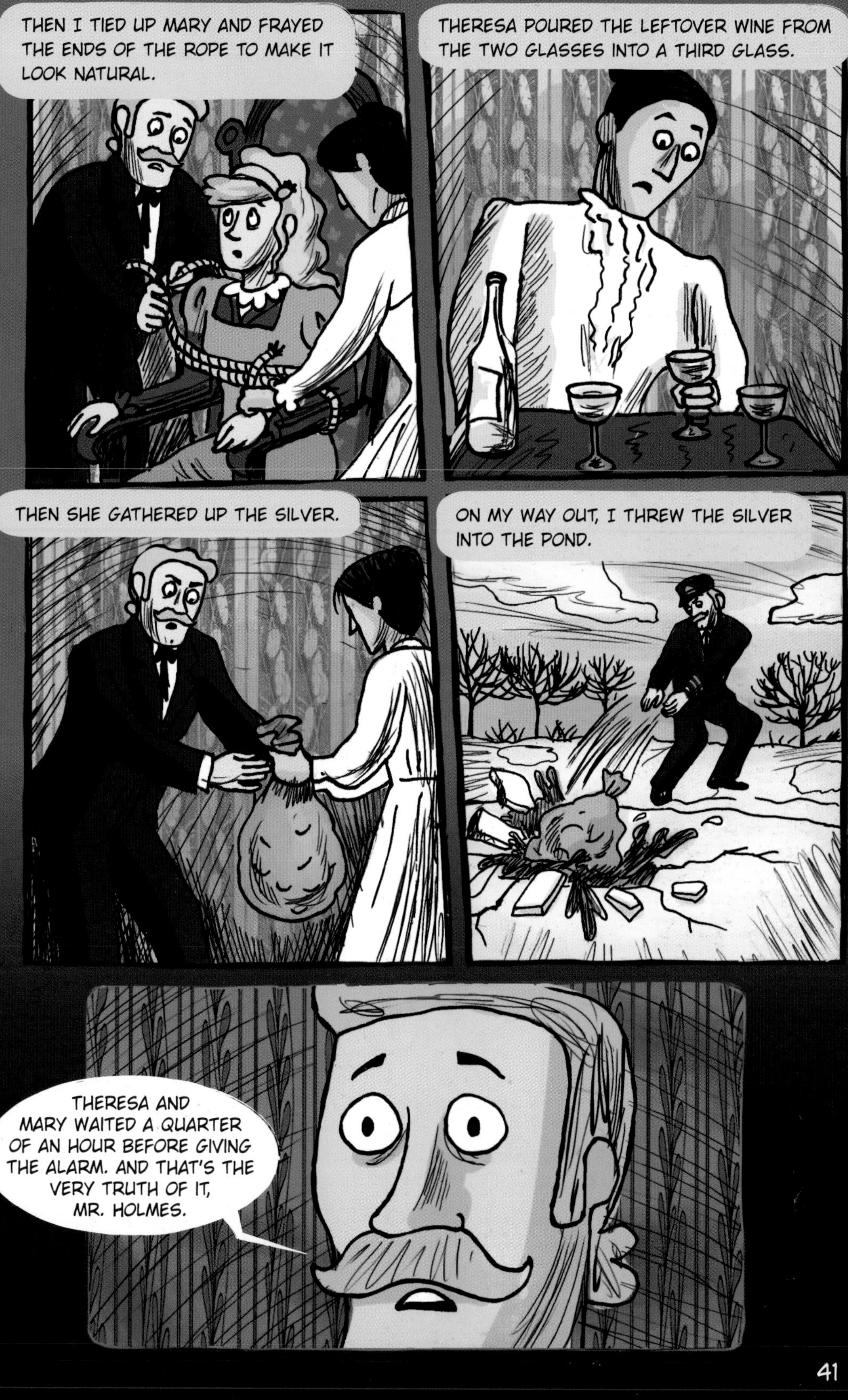
THEN I TIED UP MARY AND FRAYED THE ENDS OF THE ROPE TO MAKE IT LOOK NATURAL.
THERESA POURED THE LEFTOVER WINE FROM THE TWO GLASSES INTO A THIRD GLASS.
THEN SHE GATHERED UP THE SILVER.
ON MY WAY OUT, I THREW THE SILVER INTO THE POND.
THERESA AND MARY WAITED A QUARTER OF AN HOUR BEFORE GIVING THE ALARM. AND THAT'S THE VERY TRUTH OF IT, MR. HOLMES.

After Captain Croker finished speaking, my friend smoked his pipe for some time. The captain and I waited in silence. Then Holmes crossed the room and shook our visitor's hand.

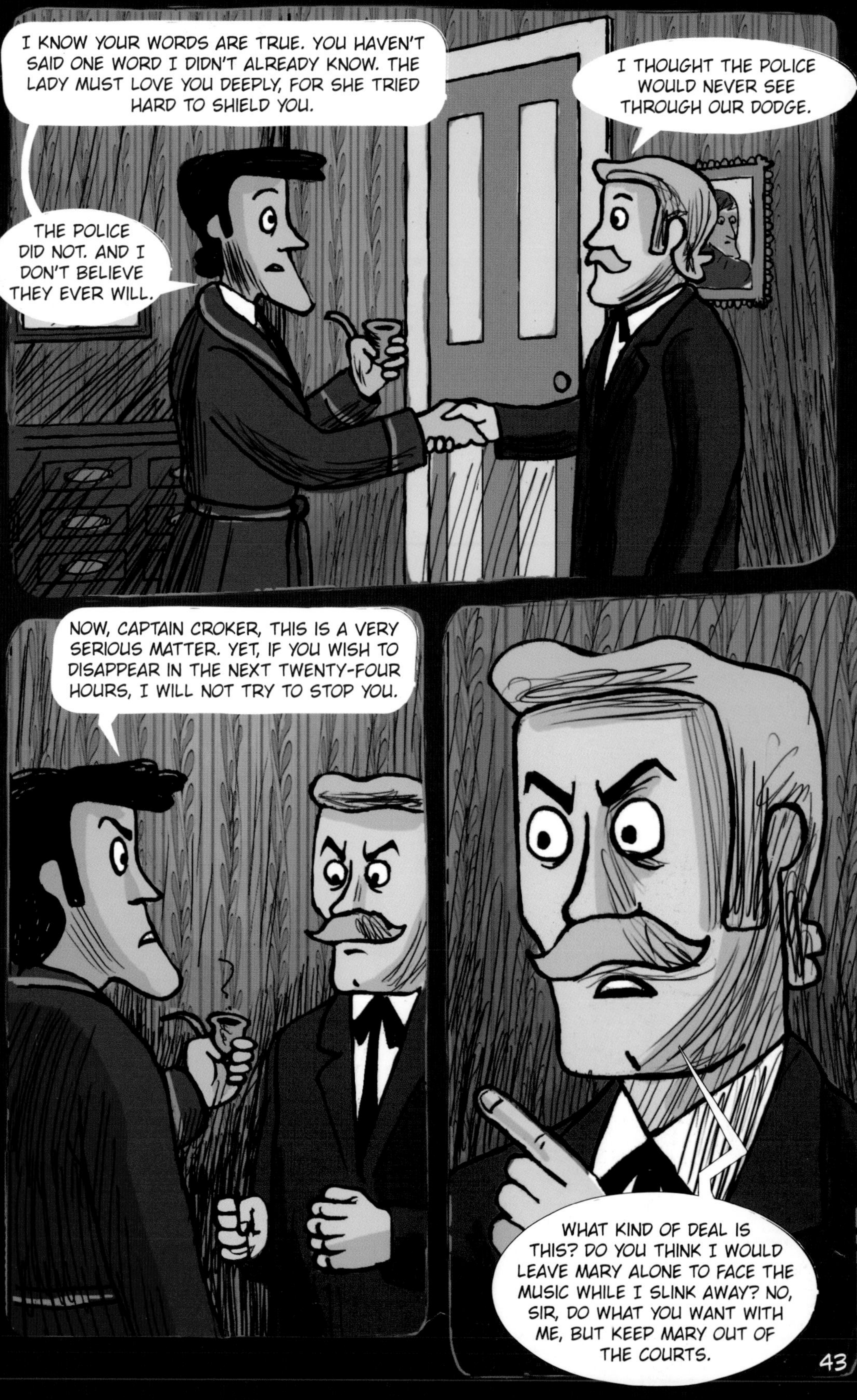
I KNOW YOUR WORDS ARE TRUE. YOU HAVEN'T SAID ONE WORD I DIDN'T ALREADY KNOW. THE LADY MUST LOVE YOU DEEPLY, FOR SHE TRIED HARD TO SHIELD YOU.
I THOUGHT THE POLICE WOULD NEVER SEE THROUGH OUR DODGE.
THE POLICE DID NOT. AND I DON'T BELIEVE THEY EVER WILL.
NOW, CAPTAIN CROKER, THIS IS A VERY SERIOUS MATTER. YET, IF YOU WISH TO DISAPPEAR IN THE NEXT TWENTY-FOUR HOURS, I WILL NOT TRY TO STOP YOU.
WHAT KIND OF DEAL IS THIS? DO YOU THINK I WOULD LEAVE MARY ALONE TO FACE THE MUSIC WHILE I SLINK AWAY? NO, SIR, DO WHAT YOU WANT WITH ME, BUT KEEP MARY OUT OF THE COURTS.

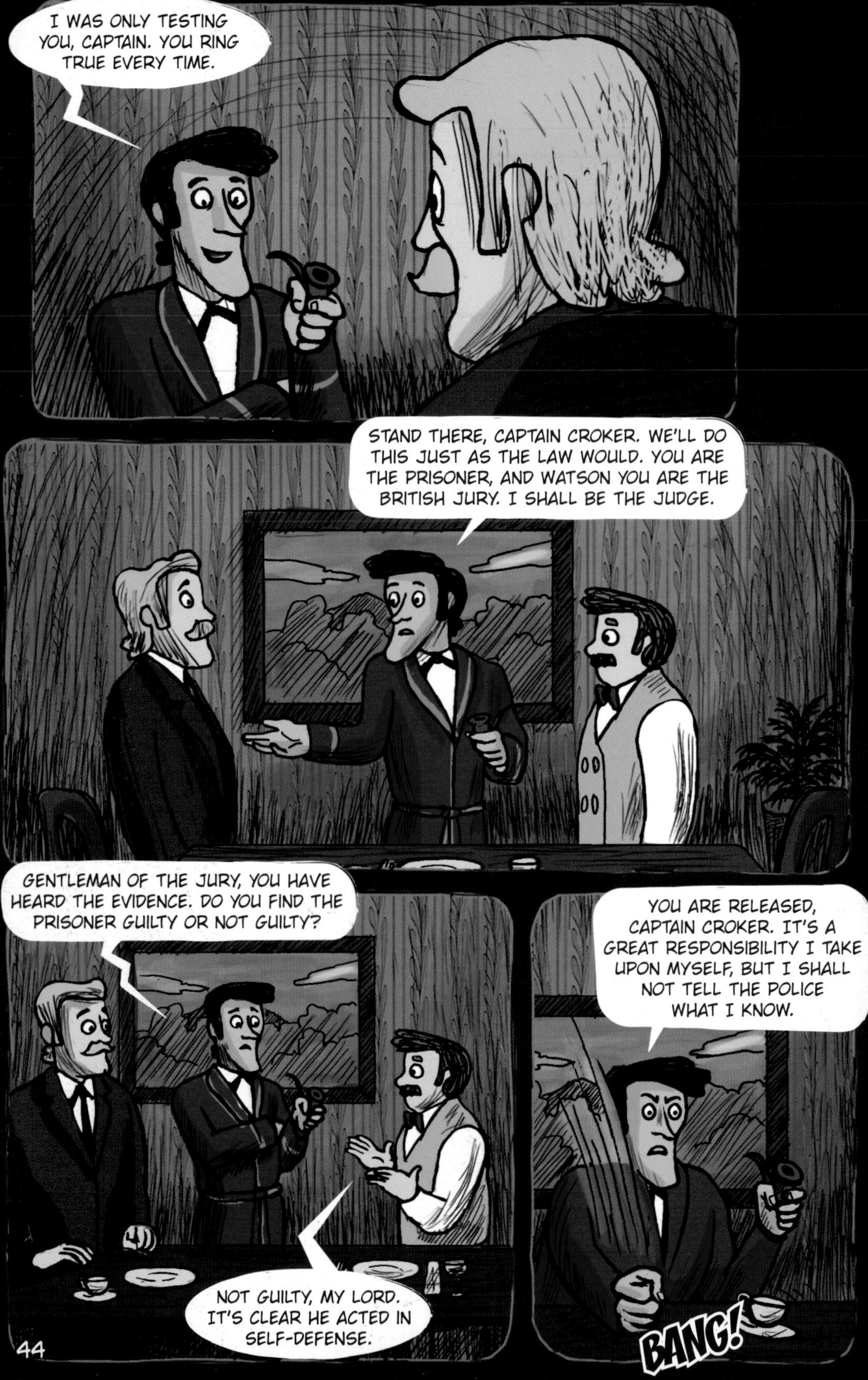
I WAS ONLY TESTING YOU, CAPTAIN. YOU RING TRUE EVERY TIME.
STAND THERE, CAPTAIN CROKER. WE'LL DO THIS JUST AS THE LAW WOULD. YOU ARE THE PRISONER, AND WATSON YOU ARE THE BRITISH JURY. I SHALL BE THE JUDGE.
GENTLEMAN OF THE JURY, YOU HAVE HEARD THE EVIDENCE. DO YOU FIND THE PRISONER GUILTY OR NOT GUILTY?
NOT GUILTY, MY LORD. IT'S CLEAR HE ACTED IN SELF-DEFENSE.
YOU ARE RELEASED, CAPTAIN CROKER. IT'S A GREAT RESPONSIBILITY I TAKE UPON MYSELF, BUT I SHALL NOT TELL THE POLICE WHAT I KNOW.
BANG!

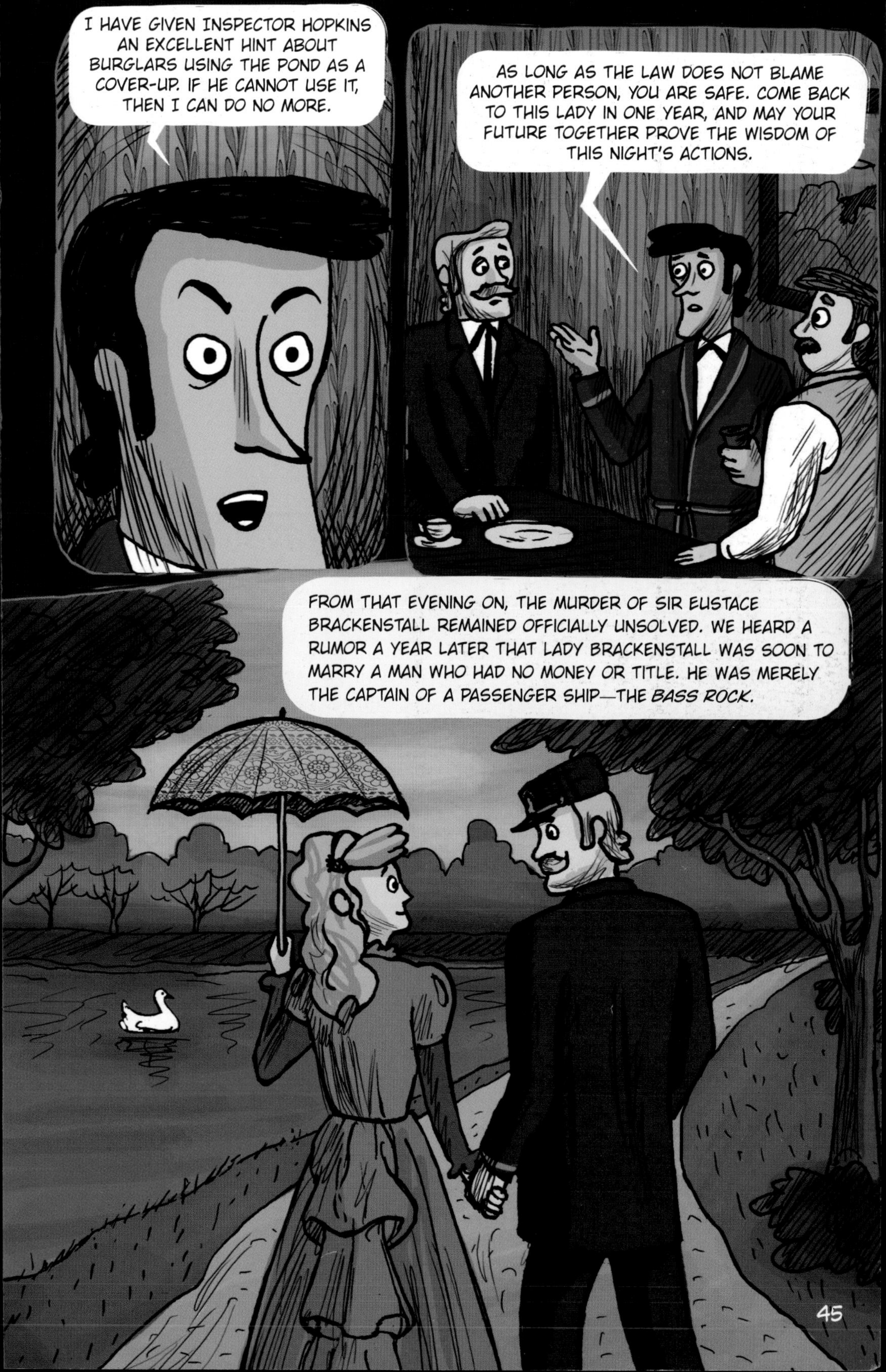
I HAVE GIVEN INSPECTOR HOPKINS AN EXCELLENT HINT ABOUT BURGLARS USING THE POND AS A COVER-UP. IF HE CANNOT USE IT, THEN I CAN DO NO MORE.
AS LONG AS THE LAW DOES NOT BLAME ANOTHER PERSON, YOU ARE SAFE. COME BACK TO THIS LADY IN ONE YEAR, AND MAY YOUR FUTURE TOGETHER PROVE THE WISDOM OF THIS NIGHT'S ACTIONS.
FROM THAT EVENING ON, THE MURDER OF SIR EUSTACE BRACKENSTALL REMAINED OFFICIALLY UNSOLVED. WE HEARD A RUMOR A YEAR LATER THAT LADY BRACKENSTALL WAS SOON TO MARRY A MAN WHO HAD NO MONEY OR TITLE. HE WAS MERELY THE CAPTAIN OF A PASSENGER SHIP—THE *BASS ROCK*.

From the Desk of
John H. Watson, M.D.

# The Adventure at the Abbey Grange: How Did Holmes Solve It?

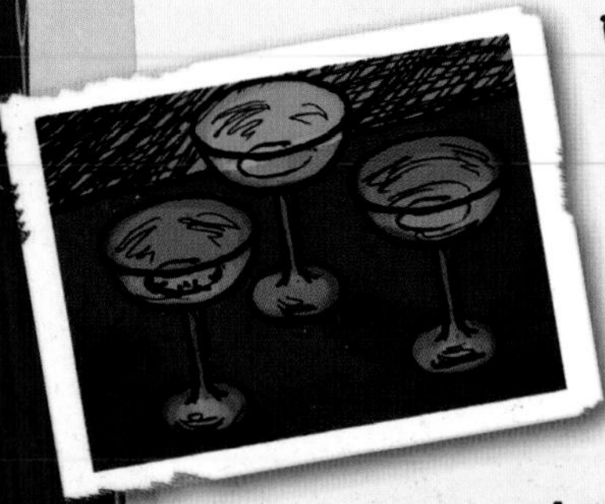

## Why did Holmes suspect that Lady Brackenstall was lying to him?

Holmes's first clue that Lady Brackenstall might be lying to him was the bent poker. The murderer had to be very powerful. Holmes did not think an elderly thief would be strong enough to deliver such a blow.

Next, only one of the three wine glasses had solid bits in the bottom. Holmes suspected that someone had poured the leftover wine from the first two glasses into the third. The bits were heavier than the wine, so they slipped more quickly out of the near-empty glasses. This left two glasses with clear wine rings at the bottom and one glass with a ring of bits. Thus, there were really only two drinkers.

Other things caught Holmes's attention. Why would the thieves leave a witness to their murder alive? Why would they use a bellpull rope to tie up Lady Brackenstall, when the bell's ringing might alarm the household? All these things seemed suspicious. So Holmes went back for another look.

## How did Holmes find out who killed Sir Eustace?

The second examination of the dining room showed that the bellpull rope had been cut rather than yanked down. Only a very tall and limber man could do the job. Holmes suspected a sailor.

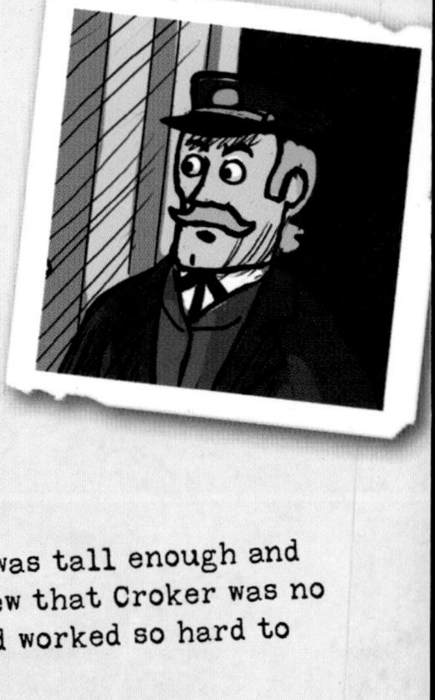

Lady Brackenstall had been around sailors a year earlier when she sailed from Australia. So Holmes checked with the shipping company. Only one sailor from her ship—the *Rock of Gibraltar*—had been in England at the time of the murder: Captain Croker. Therefore, Holmes sent the captain a telegram, asking him to visit.

## How did Holmes confirm his suspicions?

The fact that the inspector found the missing silver at the bottom of the pond proved Holmes's case. This was not a job of theft.

When Captain Croker arrived, Holmes saw that he was tall enough and strong enough to be the murderer. But Holmes knew that Croker was no ordinary murderer because Lady Brackenstall had worked so hard to protect him.

# Further Reading and Websites

Bowers, Vivien. *Crime Scene: How Investigators Use Science to Track Down the Bad Guys*. Toronto: Maple Tree Press, 2006.

Howard, Amanda. *Robbery File: The Museum Heist*. New York: Bearport Publishing, 2007.

Lane, Brian, and Laura Buller. *Crime and Detection*. New York: DK Publishing, 2005.

Petrillo, Valerie. *Sailors, Whalers, Fantastic Sea Voyages: An Activity Guide to North American Sailing Life*. Chicago: Chicago Review Press, 2003.

Sherlock Holmes Museum
http://www.sherlock-holmes.co.uk

Stetson, Emily. *40 Knots to Know: Hitchs, Loops, Bends, and Binding*. Charlotte, NC: Williamson Publishing, 2002.

Tall Ships Sailing Change
http://www.cbc.ca/kids/games/tallships/

221 Baker Street
http://221bakerstreet.org

Wilkinson, Philip. *The World of Ships*. Boston: Kingfisher, 2005.

Woolf, Alex. *Investigating Thefts and Heists*. Chicago: Heinemann Library, 2004.

## About the Author

Sir Arthur Conan Doyle was born on May 22, 1859. He became a doctor in 1882. When this career did not prove successful, Doyle started writing stories. In addition to the popular Sherlock Holmes short stories and novels, Doyle also wrote historical novels, romances, and plays.

## About the Adapters

Murray Shaw's lifelong passion for Sherlock Holmes began when he was a child. He was the author of the Match Wits with Sherlock Holmes series published in the 1990s. For decades, he was a popular speaker in public schools and libraries on the adventures of Holmes and Watson.

M. J. Cosson is the author of more than fifty books, both fiction and nonfiction, for children and young adults. She has long been a fan of mysteries and especially of the great detective, Sherlock Holmes. In fact, she has participated in the production of several Sherlock Holmes plays. A native of Iowa, Cosson lives in the Texas Hill Country with her husband, dogs, and cat.

## About the Illustrator

French artist Sophie Rohrbach began her career after graduating in display design at the Chambre des Commerce. She went on to design displays in many top department stores including Galeries Lafayette. She also studied illustration at Emile Cohl school in Lyon, France, where she now lives with her daughter. Rohrbach has illustrated many children's books. She is passionate about the colors and patterns that she uses in her illustrations.